The Empty House

Other Books by Isabelle Holland

DINAH AND THE GREEN FAT
KINGDOM

HITCHHIKE

ALAN AND THE ANIMAL
KINGDOM

OF LOVE AND DEATH AND
OTHER JOURNEYS

HEADS YOU WIN, TAILS I LOSE

THE MAN WITHOUT A FACE

The Empty House
Isabelle Holland

J. B. LIPPINCOTT   NEW YORK

Library of Congress Cataloging in Publication Data
Holland, Isabelle.
    The empty house.

    Summary: When their father is jailed for tax fraud,
no one else seems to care much, but fifteen-year-old
Betsy and her younger brother Roddy are determined to
prove his innocence.
    [1. Mystery and detective stories.   2. Fathers—Fic-
tion]   I. Title.
PZ7.H7083Em 1983   [Fic]   82-48464
ISBN 0-397-32005-1
ISBN 0-397-32006-X (lib. bdg.)

Designed by Al Cetta
1 2 3 4 5 6 7 8 9 10
First Edition

The Empty House

Chapter One

On that terrible day that my father was sent to jail, Roddy and I went to stay with Uncle Paul and Aunt Marian at their house on the Jersey shore.

"We haven't, of course, said where your father is," Aunt Marian told us. "The court hearing was in New York, and as far as I can gather, no mention was made of any connection to the summer community here. And luckily Smith is not that unusual a name." She produced a smile that wasn't a smile and said, "When a Geoffrey Smith goes to prison, as announced in papers from coast to coast and on all the national networks, it doesn't necessarily follow that Betsy and Rodney Smith are related to him. It's the first time I've been glad that my sister chose to marry anyone named Smith."

"I like Smith," I said. "People can spell it easily."

"Me too," Roddy said. "It's not stuck up."

"And anyway," I went on, "it wasn't Father's fault."

There was a silence. Then Aunt Marian said, "But it *was* his company and his responsibility, which was undoubtedly why he pleaded guilty."

"But it *wasn't* his fault." Even to me it sounded as though I was saying it more to reassure myself than because I believed it was true.

"Well," Aunt Marian said, "we won't argue about it now." She got up. "I'll show you to your rooms. Roddy, I'm afraid yours isn't much more than a closet. But it does have a window. Since Betsy is the older of the two of you, and a girl, I thought you would want her to have the better room."

"Sure," Roddy said.

Roddy is my favorite person in the whole world.

It isn't that I don't love Father a lot. Since the divorce about five years ago, Roddy and I have lived mostly with him. And I know *he* loves *us*. But he's never really needed anybody except himself and his work. And while Mother loves us, too, even before the divorce she was away a lot on assignments as a roving reporter for a news magazine. Sometimes we stayed with her and Uncle George, whom she married two years ago, which made the whole problem of schools a little difficult. But no matter where we were, and who else was or wasn't around, Roddy and I always had each other.

Roddy is very independent, but he has to have a sort of backup, and I've always been it, though it's not something either Roddy or I have ever talked about. He looks about as frail as a character in a Norman Rockwell painting: short, stocky, square face, red hair, green eyes and freckles. The all-American, all-male boy. Nothing outside shows what's going on inside. The only way I can tell is by his freckles. If they're palish, then he's okay. If they stand out like cinnamon drops, then he's upset. Roddy is twelve. I am fifteen—almost sixteen.

Before Father got zapped by the Feds, he specialized in taking over small companies that were failing, putting them back on their feet and making them prosperous, then selling them and moving on to the next failed or sinking business. Usually, he said, his first job when he took over a new firm was to fire all the M.B.A.s and efficiency experts, then get down to the nuts and bolts of how to pull the company out of the quicksands.

Father was a self-made man. He dropped out of school at fifteen (although he went back to night school later and got his high school diploma and B.S. degree), took a job in a small industrial plant and went on from there. Even the name Smith that Aunt Marian so disliked was self-made. Originally it had about five syllables, the first of which sounded vaguely like Smith, and came from somewhere far east of the river Elbe. Father immigrated to the U.S. with his parents when he was ten, and when he was excited or elated you could still hear in his voice the harsh remnants of the Silesian consonants. He married Mother, whose parents were poor but belonged to all the correct pre-Revolutionary societies, and made a lot of money. In other words, he was a smashing success until one day he found himself indicted for trying to defraud the government and, in what must have been the speediest legal action on record, sentenced to three years' imprisonment.

Everyone was stunned, Father most of all. In the few minutes we had before he was led away, he said, numbly, that he had been assured by his highly recommended lawyer that he would, of course, be fined, then receive a suspended sentence.

It didn't turn out that way at all. . . .

"Now," Aunt Marian said as we got to the top of the stairs, "this is your room, Betsy. With guests scheduled to come, I couldn't give you rooms over-looking the seafront, as I'm sure you understand. But you can just see the sea outside the side window, there, and the back is much quieter, facing into the dunes, than it is on the front with people yelling and bathing from seven o'clock on."

She went in, opened the windows and glanced around. "Everything seems to be in order. Your bathroom is next door and Roddy will be using it, too. Try not to use the other baths on this side, unless, of course, there are no guests. And even then, well, I try and keep them clean between guests, with the towels unused. Roddy, let's go to your room."

I trailed behind as we went next door. Roddy's room was small, all right. In it were a bed, a bureau, a desk and a chair. The window had an interesting view of beige sand, six garbage cans and some depressed-looking scrub grass.

Aunt Marian saw the two of us just standing there, and said, "I know it's probably smaller than you're used to, but things are going to be pretty different now. You're just going to have to accept it."

We didn't say anything. I could see the color in her cheeks.

"Okay," I said. "We accept it."

"I'm sorry. I didn't mean for it to come out like that. What I meant was—it's all happened so suddenly, and with Jenny in London and unable to get away—and not even married to your father anymore—we're all in it together."

"All right," I said. I glanced at Roddy. He looked

stolid as usual, but his freckles were beginning to stand out. "We'll make out," I said.

"Would you . . . would you like something to eat?"

"No, we ate on the plane."

"Then . . . I'll leave you. Lunch is at one. A couple of friends will be over. Your Uncle Paul may be in from the city by then, or he may not. But we do like to have meals on time so Cinda and Walter can get away for the afternoon."

"Will Cousin Bob be here?" Roddy asked.

"Robert," Aunt Marian said, with a slight emphasis, "will arrive next month. Right now he's staying with college friends."

"Oh."

"All right, I'll leave you. Better get unpacked. Don't forget. Lunch at one."

We stayed where we were, listening to her footsteps echoing on the polished wooden floor as she made her way back.

"You can have my room," I said. "She won't care."

"No. It'll be okay."

"Roddy—"

"It'll be okay," he said. "Don't hover."

"All right. I'll go and get unpacked."

My room was fairly large and square, and it had twin beds in it. Which meant that if Roddy should start feeling claustrophobic, which he does sometimes, he could easily come in and sleep in the other bed. Roddy hates all small places—closets, small rooms, elevators. The only small space he doesn't mind at all is a small car. He loves small cars.

It didn't take long to unpack. We'd been staying in Father's apartment in New York when Father was indicted. Mother had called from London and said we should leave instantly for England. But we didn't want to. Father was out on bail until the hearing and we wanted to be with him. And since Mother was up to her ears in a British election, she didn't push it.

I hung up a pair of pants, a pair of shorts and half a dozen assorted shirts and T-shirts. Along with the skirt, shirt and cardigan I had on, that would be pretty much what I'd be wearing. My two dresses and one suit I hung in the back of the closet.

At the bottom of the suitcase was a photograph of Mother and Father together. It had been taken by some street photographer on an embankment in London and he had caught them in an unposed moment. Father, with his big square head and rambunctious hair, was laughing down at something Mother had been saying. Mother, slim, good-looking, *bright*, was caught when she was talking, and it showed her liveliness and sparkle. What it didn't show was her iron determination.

I put the picture on the bureau across the room from the bed. Also on the bottom of the suitcase was a slightly smaller picture of Father. It had been taken when Father had gone down to the bowels of one of his plants, taken off his jacket and tie and decided to see if he could find out what was gumming up the innards of a large piece of machinery. There he was, with his sleeves rolled up, grease on his arm and shirt, and his hair standing practically straight up. The picture taker must have yelled, "Look up!" because he was, grinning. Propped on a piece of the machinery near him was a soda can. He looked supremely happy. That picture had been taken six months before he was arrested. I put it beside my bed.

Roddy appeared in the doorway.

"Betsy, let's go out and look at the ocean."

"All right. Where did you put your clothes?" I asked. "I didn't notice any wardrobe."

"The closet has a closet," he said. "What time is it?"

I glanced at my watch. "Ten to eleven."

"Let's go."

It was on that walk that we first saw the empty house, although of course we didn't know then that it wasn't really empty. It was a large frame house with two porches, one upstairs and one down. It wasn't even near the ocean.

We'd been walking about twenty minutes when Roddy said, "Sand, sand and more sand. Let's go inland."

So we followed a path that wound through the dunes, crossed a main road and then followed another path through some green fields and into the woods.

"Okay," Roddy said. "I'm Robin Hood and you're the sheriff coming to look for me. Give me till twenty."

So I closed my eyes and counted till twenty and then started to look for him. I finally found him, mostly because I heard him sneeze. Then I was Robin Hood and he was the sheriff. We changed roles a couple of times, and I was Robin Hood, frantically looking for a place to hide, when I broke through a knot of trees and came suddenly on the house.

It sounds funny to say "suddenly," as though it rose up before me, but it was almost exactly like that. The woods were thicker than they looked, and I didn't realize I was running towards wood-colored frame walls until I plunged through some over-grown bushes and saw the house barely twenty feet away.

I stopped cold, so that Roddy, who's always better at the game than I am, cannoned into me. "Why aren't you hiding?" he asked, and then saw the house. "Oh wow! Come on, let's go and look at it."

"No," I said. "I don't want to."

"Why not? Come on, Betsy."

"No. I don't like empty houses."

"How do you know it's empty? It may not be."

"It looks empty."

Roddy ambled over, pushing through the long, neglected grass, and started walking around the house.

I watched him go up the porch steps and try what looked like the front door. But it was locked. Then he moved over to one of the long windows and put his face close to the glass. After a minute he placed his hands on either side of his face to cut out the light.

"See anything?" I yelled.

"Just some curtains and some furniture."

He tried the window on the other side of the door, but that turned out to be even darker. Then he went back to the door. "There's no doorbell," he said.

"Probably wouldn't work if there were." By this time I'd crossed the overgrown lawn and was standing in the middle of it. I really had no desire at all to get any nearer.

"Maybe it's not the front door," he said. "Maybe it's the back one."

"What if it is? Roddy, let's go. We ought to be getting back."

"What for?" He turned and looked at me. "So Aunt Mayflower can tell us we're dirty and not up to her social standing?"

I couldn't help it. I giggled. It was a perfect name for her.

"Of course," I said, trying to find something positive to say about Aunt Marian, "she *is* descended from somebody or other who came over on the *Mayflower*. Which means that Mother is, too."

"Yeah. But Mother doesn't go on about it. Besides, it was only a cruddy boat. And the people on it were plain, ordinary people. Not Lord this and Lady that." Roddy was back at the window on the far side of the door and was peering in. "You know, Betsy, I could swear I saw something move. And I sort of *felt* it."

"What do you mean, *felt* it?"

"I mean I felt it in the soles of my shoes, the vibrations of somebody moving around."

Panic seized me. "Roddy, we have to go. It's after twelve. We have to get back. Now come on. We don't need any trouble here."

There was a silence. Finally Roddy pulled his head away from the window and came down the porch steps. "Okay," he said. He sounded surly, which meant he was disappointed. I put out my hand and squeezed his arm. He pulled it away a little. I wasn't offended, because this happened often. I'd suddenly snap the authoritative whip by reminding Roddy of something he didn't want to think about. In addition, he didn't like to be bossed, and after all I was a female. All of these things were factors, and I knew it.

"Do you mind, Your Majesty, if I go and look at the back of the house? I don't think anything can happen to me there."

"Okay. Go and look at the back and tell me what it's like."

He ran to one side of the building and looked around and then glanced back with a grin. "Only it's not the back. It's the front, with a driveway and a garage."

I went and looked myself. If anything, the house was even gloomier and more depressed-looking at the front. There was a driveway, overgrown with tufts of grass and weed. At the end of the drive was an iron gate. On either side of the gate was a jungle of trees and shrubs, which continued on the other side of the gate. Beyond the gate there was a road winding its way between the trees and bushes and disappearing around a corner some distance away.

I turned and looked at the front of the house. A fancier version of the door at the back was obviously the front entrance, now covered with dust and dirt and a few cobwebs. Rather tattered-looking blinds were visible hanging down in front of the windows. On the porch roof the gutter slanted down, broken, and the porch was filled with dirt and debris.

"This is a horrible place, Roddy. Let's go."

Roddy looked longingly at the front door. "Why don't I just give the bell a push."

"No," I said. But he was already on the porch. He never made it to the front door. There was a sound of creaking and then cracking. The floor of the porch, which was held up on the front by stilts, seemed to quiver a little.

"Get back, Roddy!" I called out.

Stubborn as always, he took one more step. There was another ominous creak.

"Roddy!" I yelled.

Then he turned. It was hard to believe that anyone as square and solid-looking could be so springy, even graceful. With one bound he cleared the porch steps and landed neatly on the lawn—or what used to be the lawn. "I'm coming."

We were late, of course.

Aunt Marian was sitting in the living room with a couple about her age. They were having drinks. "Better wash up," she said. "Lunch is ready."

When we were finally seated she asked, "Where did you go?"

I didn't know Aunt Marian too well. She had once come and stayed with us when we were in Paris, and had visited us once in London. Her voice was polite. She was carefully not showing her anger in front of the guests. But I knew she was annoyed.

"We went for a long walk on the beach," Roddy said. And since he usually prefers it if I do most of the talking, I knew that he didn't want to discuss the house we'd seen.

"How far did you go?" The man who asked was tall, thin and good-looking, with rather aquiline features.

"Miles," I said, helping Roddy out.

"I don't see how that's possible," the man said, helping himself to some salad that Walter was passing to him. Walter was a quiet, lean man. His wife, Lucinda, whom I'd seen briefly from the door, was plump, with thick hair in a bun on top of her head.

The guest, having helped himself to salad, was looking across the table at me. "At a certain point up the coast, the shoreline curves in and you come to the bay."

I decided I didn't like him. "Maybe we went in the other direction instead," I said. "We really don't know the place at all."

"Maybe," he said.

I'd been introduced to him, but I found I couldn't remember his name.

"Don't be such a legal eagle, Eric," his wife said. "Not everybody is a potentially hostile witness. You'll have to forgive my husband," she went on. "He carries his office around in his head."

"Still," Aunt Marian said, "he has a point. This house is one of only three on a point jutting out into the ocean. On either side the shoreline curves back in. I don't see how you could have walked miles."

"We were running around playing games," I explained. And then added, "Sorry to be late." I knew Roddy didn't approve of my apologizing, but I also was sure that if we didn't mind our manners, we might find ourselves on board a plane to London. In fact, the only thing that kept us here now was the fact that Mother was traipsing around Europe to get soundings from some of the Common Market countries—a subject that was looming large in the current English elections. This piece of information had come in the form of a phone call from Mother an hour or two before we arrived from New York on the plane. Aunt Marian, who disapproved of Father

but disapproved almost as much of Mother's working, had agreed to keep us for the rest of the summer.

"I see," Aunt Marian said. She then addressed
some question to Eric Whatever, and changed the
subject.

After lunch Eric and Mrs. Whatever went outside
to sit in deck chairs on the sand. Aunt Marian called
us out to the big porch, while Cinda and Walter
were cleaning the dining-room table.

"I know you've both been through a terrible
time, and for a while nothing will be easy or pleasant
for you. But—life goes on, and there still have to be
rules. So I'll lay down a few regulations that will
make things easier for all of us, and which I'll expect
you to abide by."

She paused. We stood side by side in front of her.

"All right," I said. "We're sorry about being late
for lunch. What are the others?"

"The others are that I expect you to make your
beds and pick up your clothes. Cinda and Walter will
clean your rooms, and will wash your clothes in the

washing machine in the basement along with the rest of the household laundry. If you have things that should not go into the machine, then leave them on your bed. Breakfast is at seven-thirty, lunch at one and dinner at eight. You are not to go into the kitchen. Walter and Cinda work hard and don't need to be bothered. The rules are for them more than anyone else. They have only one evening a week off, when we all go in to the village to the hotel for dinner. But they have as many afternoons off, between lunch and dinner, as they can fit into their work schedule.

"One of the pleasures of being at the shore here during the summer months is having guests, and there are nearly always some staying here. I don't want you to feel unwelcome. You're very welcome. But the rather free-and-easy existence you've always led doesn't suit this household, and I'm afraid you're going to have to conform for as long as you're here." She paused. "That's all. If you need anything, of course, just let me know."

"Thank you," I said and, since I was standing next to Roddy, nudged him.

But I knew he wasn't going to say anything, and he didn't.

Later that afternoon, when we were walking down the beach in the other direction, I said, "Roddy, try and be nice."

"Why? She didn't want us."

"Because it wouldn't take much to make her ship us to London."

"What's so bad about that? I like London—I like it a lot better than having to be with Aunt Neat and Tidy."

"If we were in London, we wouldn't be near Father."

"What good is that? How often can we see him as it is?"

"You want to see him as much as I do, and anyway, that's not the most important point. He hasn't got anybody but us. If we left he'd feel deserted."

Roddy didn't say anything; then, "Okay, so I do want to see him. But I'll bet you anything you like that Aunt Fusspot will do everything she can not to let us."

"How can she stop us? We're his children."

"Yeah? And how are we going to get there?"

"There are trains and buses and taxis."

"And who's got the money for those?"

"I do."

He turned. "You do? You didn't tell me."

"Daddy gave me some money. He said it was for emergencies."

"How much did he give you?"

I hesitated a second. Roddy was, after all, only twelve, although his thirteenth birthday was less than a couple of months away. I trusted him with anything on earth as far as his strength and courage and integrity were concerned. But he did have a big mouth when he got mad. Somebody would say something that he really didn't like, or that seemed like an attack on something or somebody he was loyal to, his wide mouth would open and out would come not only frogs and toads, but a lot of things he hadn't meant to say.

"Roddy, you must truly not tell anyone else this."

"Are you saying I'm some kind of a fink?"

"No, I'm saying that when you get riled up, you open your big mouth and all kinds of things come out. I'll tell you what Father gave me, but nobody must know. No matter what, nobody. He told me that the money he was about to give me was money he shouldn't have."

Roddy's green eyes glittered. "Father's not a thief. I don't care what the lousy newspapers said."

"Of course he's not. I'm not saying—and he didn't say—he stole the money. He just said he shouldn't have it, and might be in trouble if anyone knew he did. Okay?"

"Okay. How much did he give you?"

I cleared my throat. "Five thousand dollars."

"What?" Roddy's voice had more or less settled halfway between an alto and a baritone. Now it went sliding up into a squeak. "You've got to be kidding."

"No. It's five thousand all right."

"Where did you hide it?"

"Here." I pulled up my shirt and lifted the top of

· 25 ·

a cloth wallet that tied around my waist just below my petticoat. Then I took out five bills each marked "one thousand dollars" and bearing the picture of Grover Cleveland.

Chapter Two

Roddy gave a low whistle. "I thought the lawyer was supposed to give us money when we needed it."

"He is. But for some legal reasons I don't understand, Father's funds are being frozen, and he was afraid that the lawyer wouldn't be able to unfreeze them quickly. Everything happens so fast. There's another reason I want us to stay here," I said slowly, putting the money back. "I keep thinking we can help him somehow, maybe prove it wasn't his fault. But we have to be near him to do it."

"Betsy, I want it too. You know I do. But those lawyers he had are supposed to be among the best in the business. If they couldn't get him, well, cleared, how can we? It wasn't as if he claimed to be innocent, was it. I mean, he *agreed* that he was guilty. He said he didn't know about it, but that's not really an excuse, is it?"

Maybe that was the most awful thing of all, because it was the most unbelievable: Father, who never cheated anybody of anything, who always identified with his workers and paid them better than people doing the same jobs in other plants, finally had to plead guilty to withholding all the taxes—federal, state and Social Security—from his workers' paychecks, only not sending the withheld money on to the government; and he had to be held—and to hold himself—responsible, despite the fact that the actual man who did it was a new accountant he'd hired a few months before. Father'd never been interested in the nitty-gritty of figures—as a matter of fact, he'd never been that interested in money—and had always left that aspect of his business to accountants.

But then this nice, squeaky-clean young man got up and swore that Father—*Father*—had instructed him to cheat the government and his employees. There were no witnesses, nothing on paper. It was his word against Father's. And they took his—the accountant's—word.

Father pleaded guilty at the hearing, which meant he'd be tried by a judge instead of a jury. It seemed obvious to everyone—at least so we thought—that he was only technically implicated, and would get a whopping fine and a suspended sentence.

But it didn't work out that way. The judge bought the accountant's story. He lectured Father as though he was some greedy, insensitive moneygrubber, told him he ought to be ashamed of himself, then slammed him with the three-year prison sentence. His lawyer just sat there looking as if he'd been clobbered.

Anyway, it was as though the newspapers had been waiting for a juicy morsel like my father. He was, Father himself said grimly a few days before he was sentenced, every journalist's favorite villain: a businessman who'd done well and made money. And they really went to town on him.

There was an endless parade of headlines, stories and columns about corporate crime, how the rich steal from the poor, all portraying the businessman as the great destroyer of the American working man. Television reporters interviewed several ex-employees, all of whom were afraid they might be stuck with making up the taxes that weren't paid on their behalf, and the newsmen had a lot of fun with that. It was a few horrible weeks of hate mail, hate phone calls (until our number was changed) and being assaulted by the assembled media every time we left the apartment. Father wanted to send us down to Aunt Marian's. But we refused to go. We wanted to be with him. And I think he was glad, because he wanted to be with us too.

When it was over and the sentence had been pro-nounced, Father was given a few minutes with us before he was led away. Roddy was so stunned he said nothing. Father hugged us both. Then Roddy turned a greenish white, his freckles stood out like moles and he bolted out of the room.

"I hope he finds the men's room in time," Father said in a tired voice. Then he looked at me. "Despite everything you've heard, I had no idea that that young so-and-so was robbing both the employees and the government. Godalmighty, he comes from the same background your mother does. One of your aunt's lawyer friends knew his family. Well . . . there's nothing to be done about that now—at least for the moment." He looked down at me. "Do you really believe in me, Bits?" Only Father called me that, and it nearly broke me apart.

"Yes, Father. I do. I absolutely do."

He put his arms around me and hugged me and kissed the top of my head. "Just keep on believing in me."

I did believe him. I knew he was telling the truth. But all I could do was to hug him silently. It was then, quietly, he slipped me the envelope containing the five bills. His hand to mine. "Hide it in your bra or something," he whispered in my ear, his arms around me. "It's mine, but by rights I should have turned it over to the Feds. I had it in a desk drawer. Just keep it. We may need it."

"Where are you going to keep it?" Roddy asked now.

"In the wallet tied to my waist."

"What happens when you go in swimming?"

"I'll wrap the bills in plastic."

"But you wear a bikini."

"I'm going to get a one-piece suit. Slightly bulky." I grinned.

Aunt Marian was right about one thing. Her house was on a point that jutted out into the ocean. The point itself was about half a mile in width. On either side, the coastline curved back, and at the center of the north curve or bay was the village where people on the point did their shopping.

"I could go and get the plastic bags and the swimming suit now," I said as we reached the point.

"Using that money?" Roddy said, horrified.

"No, silly. I have my bag with me." And I did—

a small leather shoulder bag that I'd got in New York. "I still have about seventy dollars regular money and some travelers' checks."

"Okay. Maybe we can get a soda. I didn't like that lunch much."

"You wouldn't like anything Aunt Marian produced."

Roddy gave his urchin grin. "Right on."

"Why do you want to wear a swimsuit with a skirt?" the girl in the store asked. "They're for overweight ladies who're trying to hide their stomachs or their thighs."

"It's the newest thing in Cannes," I said, in my most affected accent. "Bikinis are definitely old hat. Besides, nobody size four is overweight, and that's a size four hanging there."

Grudgingly the girl let me try it on. Even four was a bit big. But I figured I could fill it up by wrapping something around me to make sure the wallet didn't fall off or get washed off, and bought the suit. The perfect "something" to wrap around me turned out to be a long thin scarf made of some synthetic material so that it would dry easily. "Is there a dime store here?" I asked the salesgirl.

"Two doors down. What do you want? Maybe we have it."

"Just some plastic—for the kitchen," I said.

"That'll be the dime store. Where're you staying?"

"With some friends."

"Oh—who?"

I hesitated and could have kicked myself. What was I trying to hide? And why? But I didn't much like the way the girl's eyes were boring into me. She wasn't a lot older than I was. "Why do you want to know?" I finally said, deciding to carry the game into her court.

"You don't believe in being friendly?" she said.

"Yes, but not in nosying into other people's business."

There were a couple of other kids who'd entered the shop in time to hear me. One of them giggled. The salesgirl flushed. "See you around," she said angrily.

I found plastic in all sizes in the small dime store,

so bought some loose sheets, plus two or three little bags. When I came out, I saw Roddy examining a paperback bookstore.

"Hi," I said. "Found anything good?"

"These." He held up a book by a famous vet, and another nonfiction book on animals. My brother adores animals. One of the frustrations of his life is that, living the way we always have, he couldn't have any. If we acquired a pet anywhere else than in England, we couldn't bring it into England without putting it in quarantine for six months. And in the flat that Mother rented pets weren't allowed.

"I'm hungry," he said when we strolled into the center of the little shopping mall. "Let's get something to eat."

We located a malt-and-burger shop and went in, and immediately saw why we hadn't encountered any boys or girls on the beach: They were all here.

Most of the kids were sitting in booths, so we edged up to the counter, where there were some seats left.

The boy behind the counter was about seventeen or eighteen, tall and rangy, with thick brown hair and gray eyes behind glasses. "What'll it be?" he said, wiping the marble counter off with a sponge.

"A vanilla shake with butterscotch sauce," I said, for want of something more inspiring. I didn't have Roddy's voracious appetite, and since Father had been arrested, such appetite as I had was inclined to come and go.

"Whipped cream and nuts?" he asked. The gray eyes behind the steel-rimmed glasses were nice, I decided. "No thanks."

He glanced at Roddy. "And you?"

"A burger and a chocolate malt."

"How do you want the burger?"

"Medium."

After a few minutes I became aware that some of the kids were covertly watching us. I could see their heads, reflected in the mirror that ran behind the counter, occasionally turning in our direction. There was a blond boy, very tanned, tall and with broad shoulders. He also appeared about seventeen. Standing beside him was a girl as dark as he was fair, and equally good-looking. Back of them, sitting in the booth, were another boy and another girl of about the same age. They were talking to one another, but they were also, every now and then, glancing in our direction.

"Just arrived?" the boy behind the counter said as he handed me my vanilla shake.

"Yes. This morning."

"Where're you staying?"

"With the MacTiernans."

"Oh." He reached behind, then turned back, holding the malt. "The burger'll be ready in a minute," he said.

There was something about his "Oh" that made me ask, "Do you know them? The MacTiernans?"

"Sure. Bob comes in here when he's home, and I see Mr. and Mrs. on my day off when I work in the garage. They bring in one of their cars to have it serviced or to buy gas."

"That's some day off," I said. "What do you do in your free time? Work in a supermarket?"

He grinned. "I don't mind. Beats lying around doing nothing."

He had a nice smile, I thought. For a minute we just stared at one another. He had the grayest eyes

I'd ever seen. Not hazel, not green, not blue. Gray.

"By the way," he said, "I'm Ted."

"Hi. My name's Betsy, and this is my brother, Roddy."

It was at that point that a shaggy-looking tan-and-black dog slipped through the door of the shop behind a customer just entering, then walked over to the end of the counter and slid around to the back.

"You know you're not allowed in here, Tiger," the boy said softly. But I saw him fish a piece of discarded hamburger from the garbage and hold it out. The morsel disappeared, and the dog wagged his tail and sat down. "Okay, if you're gonna stay, get under here." And the boy pushed the dog under a shelf carrying cups and trays of cutlery.

"That's a neat dog. Looks part shepherd and part golden," Roddy mumbled around a mouthful of burger.

"I suppose so. He was a stray when I got him."

"How old is he?"

"About five. He doesn't like being left, even when he has a yard to play in. But he's not supposed to be here. The manager is very strict about observing the 'no pets' law."

"I don't see why. Animals are cleaner than people."

"I agree. But not many would."

"Hey, Ted, is that mangy hound of yours in here?" It was the blond boy, leaning against one of the booths. "No dog meat allowed, you know."

Ted appeared not to hear. He was busy taking an order at the other end of the counter, standing, I noticed, where his feet and legs were hiding any sign of Tiger. Something made me look at Roddy. His freckles were suddenly quite brown. I debated telling Roddy to stay out of whatever was going on between the two boys, but decided that it would probably have the opposite effect.

"What a jerk," Roddy said under his breath.

"Just leave him alone," Ted said, coming back and pretending to be taking glasses out of a dryer beneath the counter. "He's showing off."

"Why?"

"Because of the new talent."

"What new talent?"

"Your sister."

"Oh." Roddy looked at me and I burst out laughing. He was always astonished when someone considered me as anything except his sister, especially if that someone obviously regarded me as good-looking. I glanced in the mirror behind the counter. Father once said to me, "I'm glad that you got your mother's looks. Old breeding in every line down to but not including your hands." He picked up one of my hands in his. "I gave you these. They come straight to you from centuries of land-working peasants." And it was true. I'm tall and thin and seem to be a collection of angles. But my hands are square, and I'm good at doing things with them—all kinds of crafts, plus the sorts of mechanical things that fathers usually teach their sons. Curiously, Roddy, for all he's so much like Father, is not as good with his hands as I am.

"Well, if that's the way he hopes to impress, he should try another tack. I like dogs too," I said.

I noticed Ted's straight eyebrows frowning over

his nose as he dealt with the glasses. "I wish he'd shut up. The manager's just come in."

I looked over at the door. A short stocky man in a business suit was glancing around the restaurant, plainly checking to make sure everything was the way it should be.

"Hey, Ted," the blond boy said. "Now about—"

"Don't I know you?" I said to him, swinging around on the stool. "You look familiar."

He strolled forward. "Now that you mention it, I'm sure we've met. It's great that you remembered." He wore a pleased grin.

Having successfully distracted his attention, I wasn't sure how to go on. Playing games—or, as my mother would call it, flirting—didn't come easily. We'd moved around too much. Not that there hadn't been one or two boys I'd admired from a safe distance. But I was always too shy to be able to do anything about it.

By this time the boy was practically at my stool.

"We have to go, Roddy," I said.

"Yeah. We sure do." He'd been glaring at the

approaching boy, but slid off his stool with great alacrity.

"Larry Babcock," the boy said, holding out his hand.

I took his hand. "Betsy Smith. And this is my brother, Roddy."

Larry said, "About that dog."

"Why don't you just shut up about that dog?" Roddy said, his face white behind the freckles. Roddy is square, but he wasn't much more than chest high to Larry.

Larry looked down at him.

"What's it to you?"

"Being mean to animals is really scummy."

"Dogs are not allowed in eating places—by law."

"Nor are people without shirts." Where I got that from I didn't know. I had no idea whether it was true or not. But it was undoubtedly true that Larry's tanned, muscular chest was bare.

He gave a slow grin.

"Yeah, but you have to consider the aesthetics of the thing."

A girl in one of the booths giggled. Roddy glared

at Larry, plainly daring him to say a word about Tiger. Ted concentrated on the glasses, which he must have gone over at least twice. Larry smiled. "How about taking in a movie later?" he said to me.

It was as neat a piece of maneuvering as I'd ever seen. If I said no, he'd almost certainly go on talking about Ted's dog. Roddy and I had revealed our colors as pro-dog.

"You don't have to go out with him just to save Tiger," Ted said.

"What's this 'have to'?" Larry asked. Obviously self-doubt was not a part of his character. He was now lolling back against one of the counter stools, his thumbs in his jeans belt, his upper body a golden brown, lightly sprinkled with sand, the muscles of his arms going in and out in exactly the right places.

"Put on your shirt, Larry," the manager said, walking up behind us. "You know we don't allow that in here."

For a moment Larry just looked at him out of his cool blue eyes, then he reached over the partition of a booth and pulled up a handful of material that turned into a dark-blue T-shirt. "Just to accommodate you and the ladies," he murmured, and slipped it on. Then he leaned back to look over his shoulder at the area behind the counter where Tiger was hiding. Having made this point, he straightened and said to me, "About that movie—"

"Come on, Tiger. You know you're not allowed in here," Ted said, and dragged the reluctant dog by his collar from beneath the shelf, out into the main part of the restaurant and towards the door.

"I've told you a dozen times," the manager yelled, "not to let that dog in here. It's against the law and it's not sanitary. If I catch him in here again, you're fired. Do you hear me—fired."

Ted got Tiger through the door, turned his nose towards the center of the town and patted his behind, pointing with his hand. What he was saying was plain—"Home."

Tiger sat down, flopped his face on his paws and looked pathetic. Ted came back in.

"Did you hear me?" the manager yelled. "I told you—"

"Yes, I heard you. If I bring Tiger in here again, I'll be fired. Message received and over." He got behind the counter and started clearing off the dirty crockery.

There was a dead silence. Nobody said anything. The manager, red in the face, stalked towards the back of the store and through a door.

Roddy turned towards Larry. "You really are a pile of manure. You stink."

Larry looked at him and then shrugged. "It's not my law. And as long as you're the size of a fireplug, you can get away with saying that, as I'm pretty sure you knew before you said it. There's nothing like being a hero when you're safe."

I knew right away I should have got Roddy out of there earlier. But even so, I didn't move fast enough. There was a blur, and then I saw Roddy's fists pummeling Larry's midriff and a knee coming up to inflict damage in an even more vulnerable area.

"Roddy, stop." I yelled and sprang, getting my arms hooked into his and pulling back as hard as I could.

Suddenly Ted was between Larry and Roddy. "Only creeps bait children and animals," he said.

Larry turned. "Watch your mouth, boy. You might get a fist down it."

"I might get one down yours instead."

Larry moved towards the counter.

"Ted . . ." I said, not entirely sure how I was going to go on.

But at that point the fight was interrupted. "I thought we might find you here, among the other boys and girls. Hello, Larry, how nice to see you. How are your parents?" And Aunt Marian, looking both cool and well dressed in white linen, with her tanned feet slipped into espadrilles, was walking across the floor with her eyes on Larry and her hand out. And the manager was hurrying from the back, a big grin of welcome on his face.

Chapter Three

I couldn't believe Aunt Marian hadn't heard or seen through the glass panels in the front of the store the fracas immediately before her entry. But apparently she hadn't. Shaking Larry's hand, she said in a voice oozing with goodwill, "Robert's coming early next month. I know he'll be glad to see you."

Roddy said in a low voice, barely moving his lips, "In that case, he has to be a creep."

"Shut up," I replied, equally *sotto voce.* "We're in enough trouble." As I spoke, I glanced outside.

Tiger was lying on the sidewalk, head on paws, still acting like a waif. I looked behind the counter. Ted had disappeared. In his place was another boy, thin and dark. Then Ted, in T-shirt and jeans, walked past us to the door.

"Quittin' already?" Larry said, grinning.

"It's past his regular time," the manager said quickly. He glanced at a big clock on the wall. "Half an hour past. See you tomorrow at eight." There was a conciliatory note in his voice that surprised me.

"And don't bring the wildlife," Larry said as Ted went through the door.

"He won't," the manager put in hastily. "It's just that the dog sometimes comes to pick him up."

"Dogs have no place where food is being prepared," Aunt Marian said.

I was standing right by Roddy and took hold of his arm.

"We don't need any more trouble," I whispered. "And we don't need to make trouble for Ted and Tiger." I wasn't at all sure the first would have much power with him. But the second might, and evidently did. I saw the stubborn look come over his face, but he kept his mouth shut.

"I came to see if you wanted a swim," Aunt Marian said. "If so, I want you both to go in while Eric's still here. There are guards on the beach, of course—Larry here is one—but you should get a feeling of the surf before you go in by yourselves. So I drove into the village to get you. You brought swimsuits, of course."

"Yes," I said.

"All right. Let's go. Larry, won't you join us?"

My finger coiled against Roddy's arm. But he had apparently decided for himself that any more obstreperousness would be counterproductive, because he just stared straight ahead through the glass front to where Ted and Tiger were walking across the mall.

"No thanks, Mrs. MacTiernan. I have to be on guard duty later this afternoon, so I think I'll hang around here till then." He glanced at me. "See you around."

"Good-bye," I said, my eyes on Ted's retreating figure.

I went to change as soon as we got back, wrapped the wallet and then the scarf around my waist and then slipped on the suit.

"Good God," Aunt Marian said when I appeared, "don't you have something a little younger than that? Is that what they're wearing in Europe now?"

"It's the latest thing at Cannes," I said.

Eric's wife, Lynn, was eyeing my suit. "Then it can't be the super-chic Cannes we've all come to know and hate—the one that gives all its awards to anti-American movies."

I giggled before I could stop myself. My own view of Cannes was not far removed from hers. If I'd met her somewhere else, under different circumstances, I would have liked her. As it was, I said, "The same."

Lynn looked at the suit a long time and then at me. "Whatever you say," she said.

"Well, I think it's a disgrace," Aunt Marian said. "I'll see to it that you'll have a new suit tomorrow."

"But I like this, Aunt Marian. I like it very much. I don't want a new suit. Thanks just the same."

Roddy was listening to all of this with a broad grin. He'd put on his red trunks, and his body rose tanned and sturdy above that.

"Let's go in," he said, and ran towards the water, ignoring Aunt Marian's opening remarks on the surf. I was prepared for her to have made a fuss over nothing about the dangerousness of the water, but was surprised to find that there was indeed a powerful undertow. Fortunately, both Roddy and I had been swimming since we were babies, so it didn't frighten us.

But as we were coming out of the water, something made me say, "Roddy, you took your medicine this morning, didn't you?"

"Stop clucking like a hen," Roddy said in a surly voice. "I don't want the world to hear about it."

"There's nobody within fifty feet of us, and anyway, I kept my voice down. You did take it, didn't you?"

"Yes, I took it. End of subject." And he stalked away. Of all the many things I could do that he loathed, reminding him of his medicine and, by implication, his illness, was the most abhorred.

Sometimes, I thought, watching Roddy's straight back ahead of me, you can't win.

I should have known that Aunt Marian wasn't the type to give up easily. The next morning at breakfast she said, "I'm taking you down to the village, Betsy. The sports shop is small, but they always have a good selection of suits."

"But I like my suit," I said.

"If you really like that suit at your age, then I think you might need a therapist as much as you need a new bathing suit."

"Betsy doesn't need a therapist," Roddy said belligerently. "A doctor once said that Betsy was probably the only really well balanced person he'd ever met."

"Then why does she want to wear a bathing suit that makes her look like a grandmother?"

"That's—"

"Roddy!" I almost shouted his name. "Thanks, but it's okay. I'll get the suit. It's not that big a deal." I added that as slowly as I could, so he'd get the emphasis and translate correctly that I wasn't that upset by Aunt Marian's edict.

"What about the money?" he whispered to me after breakfast.

"The surf is so strong, I think maybe my idea of wearing it around my waist wasn't so hot."

"Where're you going to put it, then?"

"I don't know. Let's see if we can think of a place."

"The empty house," Roddy said promptly.

"You would say that! No. If I ever need it, I might need it fast. It's got to be somewhere close to hand."

At the last moment Roddy refused to go with us, so Aunt Marian and I set out in the big Cadillac, riding in the back behind Walter.

I expected to have trouble with the girl in the store, and when she caught sight of me, her face did, for a moment, freeze. But she was so busy being gracious to Aunt Marian that it was almost unnoticeable.

"How can you have sold her such a ludicrous bathing suit?" Aunt Marian said.

"I told her how stupid it was, and how it made her look like an old lady, but she insisted on having it." And the girl's light-brown eyes fixed themselves on me, as though challenging me to argue with her. "She said," the girl went on, obviously enjoying herself, "that it was the latest fashion in Cannes."

"Well, I don't know what was going on in her mind," Aunt Marian said, "but bring us out some suits that are about fifty years younger."

They were both, I thought crossly, talking about me as though I was a blot on the wall.

"Try this on," Aunt Marian said, when the salesgirl had brought out an armful of suits.

It was on the tip of my tongue to say, You're arranging and dictating all this, why don't you try it on?

"All right," I said meekly, and went into the dressing room. Before I changed, I put the wallet in my small shoulder bag. I would really have to find a place for it back at the beach house, I thought.

To my irritation the suit was perfect—a blue-and-green bikini that covered enough, but not too much, and that looked smashing against my tan.

"Come out and let us see you," Aunt Marian called out. So I did.

"That's more like it," she said when I appeared. "Cannes, indeed! I never heard such nonsense. Well, we'll take that and one more. Pick out another one, Betsy."

"How about this?" I said, holding up a one-piece that looked about the size of an envelope.

"I don't know where you get all this Puritan ethic from," Aunt Marian said.

"Actually, Mrs. MacTiernan, that's the newest thing. One-piece suits, ones that *fit*," the salesgirl said with a glance at me, "are terrifically in."

So I had my one-piece suit after all.

"Thank you, Aunt Marian," I said as we came out. "That was nice of you." Why was it so hard to say those words?

"You're very welcome," she said, sounding as stiff as I felt.

As we faced the mall, I saw Roddy playing some kind of game with Tiger. "May I go over to the burger shop and have a milk shake?" I asked.

"Of course. You don't have to ask my permission

for everything you do. Just remember, lunch at one." And she got into her car and was driven away.

I walked slowly towards Roddy and Tiger. "You got here pretty fast," I said.

"It isn't far. I just ran along the beach and back around the bay. Isn't he a neat dog?"

Tiger, who looked about five years younger now that he was playing games, wagged his tail and jumped up on me. "Yes indeed. Tiger, you're a thing of beauty and a joy forever," I quoted. Then I nodded towards the shop. "Are all the kids in there?"

"Yeah, the same crowd as yesterday. I wonder if they ever swim. Wanna go in?"

"No." It was strange how strongly I felt about that. I would have liked to see Ted again, but I didn't feel too much like coping with Larry. "Let's go home, Roddy. Come help me find a place to put this money."

"Okay. I wish we could take Tiger."

"Well, we can't. I have a feeling that the manager and Aunt Marian are soul mates as far as dogs go."

"Yeah. All right, old man, we'll be back." He rumpled Tiger's ears and then followed me.

We were walking past the burger shop when a voice said, "Betsy, Roddy."

We turned. Ted was standing at what was obviously the burger shop's side door, shoving a big black plastic bag into the garbage can. "Hi," he said.

"Tiger looks terrific this morning," Roddy said.

Ted grinned. "He should. I gave him a bath last night—in your honor."

"Can I take him for a short run down the beach?" Roddy asked.

"Sure, don't worry. You can't lose him. He'll find his way back."

Roddy and Tiger took off.

"Doesn't he have a dog of his own?" Ted asked me.

"No. We've moved around too much. And we're in England a lot. If you live there, you can't bring an animal in without putting him in quarantine for months."

"Yeah, I know. That's too bad. Although they're

right about the quarantine. England's practically the only European country without rabies."

I looked at him. Not too many people knew this. "Have you been there?"

"Yes. Last year. Maybe when you settle down, he can get a dog. Are you here for keeps?"

It was a funny question. No one had ever asked it that way before. "We're never anywhere for keeps," I said. There was a silence. Then I looked at him. "But I wish we were. Do you live here all year around?"

"No. I live in Westchester."

"Ted!" The voice came from the restaurant.

"Look," Ted said hurriedly, "can you—"

"Hey, Ted, where are you?"

"A movie? Tuesday night?" Ted said.

"Sure. Okay."

"Ted! Where the. . . ." The manager's head looked out.

"Just putting out the garbage," Ted said.

The manager stared at me. "You're Mrs. Mac-Tiernan's niece, aren't you?"

"Yes."

"Well—come in." He smiled. "We're happy to have you. Larry and the others are inside."

Out of the corner of my eye I saw Ted's hand wave as he disappeared. "I will, thanks, but not now. I have to get back to the house." The manager nodded at me and followed Ted.

Roddy came bounding up with Tiger. "He's a super dog."

"Well, leave Superdog now and come and help me find a place for the money."

We walked in silence for a while. I was thinking about Ted, and Roddy was (I was sure) thinking about Superdog, when I saw him glance over his shoulder.

"I think your hot lover is following you," he said, and by the tone of his voice I knew he couldn't be talking about Ted.

"Who?" I said, and turned.

Larry Babcock waved and started to lope towards us. "Hi," he said. "How about that movie we were talking about? There are a couple of good ones in the next town, and if you don't like those, there are about six on the boardwalk farther north."

"Thanks a lot," I heard myself say, "but Aunt Marian has some people coming over tonight. Another time, maybe. Come on, Roddy, let's race." And I took to my heels, with Roddy pounding beside me. After a few seconds of that, I turned around and waved. I didn't want to seem too offputting. He was standing where we'd left him, his hands on his hips. The sun was shining against his face, and at that moment it didn't look very pleasant. Ignoring my wave, he turned and started back towards the mall.

"How long do we have to keep on running?" Roddy panted beside me as I took off again.

"Until we round the point," I said.

Then we walked in silence for a bit. I was still trying to figure out why I'd put Larry off again. It certainly wasn't that he failed a looks or charm test. He had plenty of both. I found him arrogant and phony, though. Partly it was Roddy, too. If I went out, what would happen to him? There didn't seem to be many kids his age on the beach or in the village. Of the dozen or so young people I'd seen, most were, if anything, older than I was. I glanced sideways at Roddy. He was pacing for-

wards, his lips compressed, his eyes on the breakers that flowed in and sprawled on the sand. On
the other hand, I thought, with all these concerns
about Roddy, I had accepted Ted's invitation fast
enough!

My preoccupation with Roddy seemed to be
more urgent here than it had been elsewhere. Was
it because Father was in prison and I felt somehow
that this meant we had to close ranks? Put that way,
the whole idea seemed crazy. And yet . . . deep
down, and very seriously, I felt that I couldn't just
abandon Roddy to his own devices. It wasn't that I
thought he would have a seizure—he hadn't had one
in almost two years. The doctor back in England was
talking about phasing Roddy off his medicine. And
it wasn't that I thought he'd get into trouble or do
something wrong. . . . But when I had examined—
and rejected—all my feelings about *not* leaving
Roddy alone, I was still left with the feeling itself—
as strong as ever.

Explaining it to Aunt Marian was something else.

"Larry called," she said, just as we walked in before lunch. "He wanted to know if he could drop

over this evening—and if maybe he could take you to a movie."

"What did you say?" I asked. I wondered if he'd told Aunt Marian my fictitious story about the people she wanted me to meet. If he had, then I was going to be in more trouble.

"I said I'd ask you."

"Aunt Marian," I said. "I really don't much want to go out with him."

"Why on earth not? I'm sure you gathered from what I said to him that he's a good friend of Robert's. And he comes from a nice family—one of the best in the summer community. Furthermore," she said slowly, "I have the distinct impression that there's not a girl around who wouldn't give anything to be asked out by him. I can't understand you. Heaven knows, he's good-looking."

"Yes, he is. I just don't like him very much."

"Why not?"

"I didn't like his attitude towards Ted, the boy behind the counter. He sort of baited him."

"Well," Aunt Marian said, "I wouldn't concern

myself too much with little rivalries among the boys. Ted's probably jealous and shows it. Ted's a nice enough boy, and he certainly works hard, but he's not one of the group at the Club, and I think he may give himself airs."

"It's the other way around," Roddy said. "Larry acted like he owned the place."

Aunt Marian's nostrils flared a little. Until that moment she'd seemed fairly reasonable. But the steel hand became suddenly visible. "For all we know, he does—or his father does. Larry Senior owns a lot of property, including some shopping malls. What did you two do this morning?" The change of subject was abrupt.

"We took a walk on the beach," I said.

"Speaking of the beach, there's always supposed to be a guard on duty. Was there? I was inside all morning and didn't notice."

As a matter of fact, there hadn't been. The big chair about a hundred yards down from the house had been empty. "No, there wasn't, I don't think."

"That's why I brought it up. I want the two of you

to promise me that you will not go in unless either there's somebody on guard duty or one of us is going in at the same time. Promise?"

"All right, we promise," I said. I couldn't forget how powerful the undertow was. "Come on, Roddy, promise. Please."

Roddy was wearing his stubborn look. "It seems silly if the ocean is right there—" he started.

"Roddy," I said. "Come on!"

"Oh, all right, Miss Fuss E. Pot."

Aunt Marian's face relaxed into a smile. There were moments when she reminded me of Mother in one of her sunnier moods. Then she turned to me. "I still don't know why you don't want to go out with Larry. I told him as far as I was concerned he was certainly welcome to come here, and the rest would be up to you."

I spent the time immediately after lunch trying to decide where to hide my five thousand dollars. If I put it under the mattress, then Cinda might find it when she was changing the bed linen. If I put it in a drawer or in the medicine cabinet in the bathroom, anyone might find it. There were no loose boards, either in the room or in the closet. I finally decided to put the five bills in an envelope and tape the envelope to the underside of one of the bureau drawers. It wasn't guaranteed safe, but it was better than anything else I could think of. But that meant I had to go back to the village to get the envelope and the tape.

"Let's go to the village," I said to Roddy.

"I'm tired of that place."

"You might see Tiger again."

Roddy compressed his lips and stared at me. "Okay. But afterwards I want to go back and look at that house. If you don't want to come with me, it's all right. But I'm going."

"Roddy, I really don't like that place. It's spooky."

"You don't have to come with me. But I'm going to go and see what's inside."

I debated using one last weapon: Don't go there, Roddy—for me. I'd used it once or twice before in our lives together, and it had worked. But he deeply resented it, and I didn't blame him. It was a ploy that Mother used from time to time, and I hated it as much as Roddy did. It's the original no-win position. If I knuckle under, I feel rotten and angry. If I don't knuckle under, I feel guilty and angry.

"Okay," I said. "But come into the village with me first. As I said, you might see Tiger."

"Much good that'd do me. I wish I could have a dog of my own."

For the first time, I wondered if I was wrong about insisting on being here. If I even half suggested it, Roddy would be on the plane to London. But my own growing need to be close to Father had become more important than anything else.

"You look like you're doping out how to put the atom back together again," Roddy said. "What're you thinking about? How to get Dad out of the pokey?"

Sometimes, I thought, it was really uncanny how closely our minds worked. "You should look into doing one of those so-called magic acts," I said irritatedly. "You know the kind—'I have here in my hand a sealed envelope. The note inside it reads . . .' et cetera, only you'd be blindfolded."

Roddy grinned. "I just know you! There's Tiger.

You go and get whatever you have to get, and I'll go play with him."

We went to the empty house later that afternoon, with me trailing beside Roddy as though I were excess baggage.

"I told you, you don't have to come with me," Roddy said.

"It's okay. You've made me curious."

Half an hour later we were standing at the edge of the clearing.

"I don't know why you want to have anything to do with it," I said. "It's so gloomy."

"So go back," Roddy said, and walked up to the rear door. For a while he stood peering into the windows, his hands shielding his eyes from the light. Then, without any warning, he went and knocked loudly on the long glass panel of the door.

We both waited—he up on the porch in front of the back door, I on the ground a dozen feet away. There was no reply. Maybe, I thought, the gods are with me. Roddy knocked again, this time against the wooden lintel—a loud tattoo. Again, there was no answer.

"Come on, Roddy," I called, trying not to sound too happy. "Nobody's there."

"Yes there is," he said. "And they're coming to the door."

Although I felt as though some giant hand was trying to keep me away from the house, I went up the steps and stood beside Roddy. He was right. Someone was coming. We couldn't see anything about the person, because the glass was frosted. But I could see the shape slowly growing. And then the door opened. I could feel my heart beating wildly. What did I expect—some kind of monster?

The reality was tame. It took me a minute to realize I was looking in the wrong place for somebody's face: it was lower than I expected. The reason was that the woman was in a wheelchair. As the door swung open, somebody called from inside.

Obviously the shouted, indistinct words had been a question. The woman in front of us called back, "No, Mother. It's two children. What do you want?" she asked us. It was a perfectly polite question. But there was something about the way she asked it that sounded wary, withdrawn.

"Er—we thought the house was empty," Roddy said.

"Then why were you banging on the door like that? Who are you?"

"I'm Elizabeth Smith," I said as firmly as I knew how. "And this is my brother, Roddy."

A strange smile touched the woman's face. For a moment she looked almost beautiful. "I used to know somebody named Smith," she said. "He was wonderful. A knight in armor!"

One of the troubles with being named Smith is the response people have when you tell them. One tried-and-true witticism is: "Smith? I knew somebody named Smith once, in New York City. Ha-ha!" I sometimes wonder if the Joneses and the Browns have the same trouble.

"How nice," I said sarcastically.

"Come in," she said gaily, and wheeled her chair around.

Chapter Four

We stepped into the hall, and she closed the door behind us. Roddy and I stood there in the hall, a little stunned, staring around us.

The place was like a combined antique shop and zoo. The furniture was elegant and looked old, but it was scattered around in a higgledy-piggledy way, and there was a lot of it. In the hall was a huge oblong mirror with a gilt frame, and a little table attached to the wall, with two curved legs, meeting in the center, and feet shaped into great claws around a ball. There were three chairs and one stool with torn red-velvet seats; two little bureaus side by side, one with a marble top; and an old hat stand, with shawls and sweaters draped over it. Every space not occupied with furniture was covered with bookshelves filled with books—books standing up, books lying down, books lying on top of the rows and books here and there stacked up horizontally acting as bookends to other books.

Prominently displayed were three cats, one on each of the chairs, and on the stool a large brown-and-white guinea pig, and in a cage hanging by a rope from the ceiling, a parakeet. There was a powerful animal smell.

"Who are you?" the parakeet jabbered. "Go away, go away."

"Stop it, Toby, you're being rude," the woman said.

"Hey, that's a neat bird." Roddy went over and stared up at the cage. "Hi, Toby. How are you?"

"None of your business," Toby said. His funny curved beak twisted this way and that. "Go away."

"He really understands," Roddy said, delighted.

"Of course," the woman said. "Did you think he wouldn't?"

"No. I think animals understand just as much and are a lot nicer than people—most people," Roddy ended diplomatically.

The woman looked at him gravely for a moment. "You are worthy of being a Smith," she finally said. "Come and meet Mother."

She wheeled her chair through a doorway at the left. "I've brought you two visitors," she called out.

It was a huge room, also crammed with furniture, some of which stood in little islands in the middle. An enormous oriental carpet, worn almost threadbare, covered about half the floor, and the rest of the floor was bare, the wood dull and scuffed. Books climbed the walls here, too, and an ancient patterned wallpaper covered the few spaces not occupied by furniture and bookshelves. Inappropriately, a strong, ugly modern light dangled from the ceiling. The animal smell was even more powerful here, and there were more animals: Another guinea pig sat in a cage on the floor, methodically chewing lettuce. There were, at first sight, at least four more cats, two magnificent white angoras, a large ginger tom and a small black female. In the middle of the floor, making its slow way across the carpet, was a tortoise.

Roddy's face caught my eye for a moment. He looked as though he had, quite by accident, happened on the Kingdom of Heaven. It suddenly occurred to me how rarely I'd seen him look that way. So much of his life had been spent building defenses: defenses against the humiliating and unpredictable onslaughts of his illness, against a family situation that had come unstuck, against too many schools and new classmates who could be cruel.

"Hey," he said, stroking the white cat nearest to him. "What's your name?"

"His name is Ozymandias," an imperious voice said from the corner of the room. " 'My name is Ozymandias, king of kings: look on my works, ye Mighty, and despair!' "

We both turned. We hadn't seen her before, because her back was to one of the long windows. Sun streamed through the windows onto her and over her shoulders, putting her face in shadow. But I could see that she and the armchair in which she was sitting made a considerable bulk.

"What are your names?" the same imperious voice said.

"My name is Roddy," Roddy said. "This is my sister, Elizabeth."

"You like animals?"

"Yes, more than anything."

There was an electric silence, almost as if the two of them were the only people in the room. I moved slightly, so that the sun didn't blind me. And I saw her then more clearly: gray hair piled in a bun, a proud, hooked nose, dark eyes peering out from under straight brows. It was a fierce, patrician face, reminding me of portraits I'd seen in museums. For a moment more she and Roddy looked at one another. I had a queer feeling that they saw things in each other that we couldn't see. It was like watching a friendship happen.

"And the other white cat is named Bianca," the old woman said.

"What are your names?" I asked. After that silence, the words sounded rude and brusque.

"I'm Ellen Whitelaw," the old woman said. She glanced at the younger woman in her wheelchair, who had taken the guinea pig out of the cage, lettuce and all, and was quietly talking to it. "This is my daughter, Miranda."

"And this is Sebastian," Miranda said. "I think he's getting tired of lettuce."

I noticed the crutches then, propped to the side of the dark-red armchair on which Ellen sat. It was a warm day, and the windows were closed, which probably accounted for the strength of the aroma. But a light robe covered the older woman's legs.

"We are recluses," Ellen said. "We don't bother other people, and we don't want them to bother us."

Roddy, who was squatting on the floor, looking at the tortoise, started, "Can't we—" He sounded anxious.

"I should have said most people," Ellen went on.

"We don't like this century," Miranda said in a dreamy voice. "So we don't bother with all those nasty things that people have in their houses—at least, we hear they do."

"What nasty things?" I asked.

"Radio, television, telephone," Ellen said. "And we don't read newspapers. We have more than enough to read here." She swung her arms around the room. As she did so, she knocked something to the floor that had been on a wooden board across her lap. I moved across and picked it up. It was graph paper. On the paper was an illustration of many animals and many plants. I saw that, propped on an easel beside the chair, was the original, a painting in oils of a scene that could easily be called "The Peaceable Kingdom." The trouble was, the painting was not at all good, and the animals were barely recognizable. The plants were slightly better, but not much.

"That's Miranda's work," Ellen said, watching me.

I glanced down at the drawing. "What are you doing?" I asked.

"Making it into a needlepoint pattern."

I saw then the bags around the bottom of the chair, containing wools of various colors, plain canvases and some stamped with illustrations.

"I invent illustrations and then send them to somebody who sells them," she said.

"You don't have television?" Roddy asked, horrified.

"No." Ellen picked up a crayon and started working with her drawing. "If we don't like modern life, why should we import images of it into our home?"

"This is our castle," Miranda said in her dreamy voice. "With its invisible moat."

"Castle?" I said, and thought, This dust-ridden old ruin?

"You have to learn to see the reality behind the appearance," Ellen said. "That's what life is all about." She looked at me and then at Roddy. "It takes time, and a great deal of determination, but it can be done. Yes, Bagheera, you may come in."

She added that in such a natural voice that I fully expected to see someone else walk in. Which is, of course, what happened, except that the someone else was an enormous black cat with tilted green eyes, high back legs and a voice that bespoke its Siamese ancestry.

Bagheera, after completing a stately circle, suddenly jumped up into Ellen's lap, onto her board, sweeping more bits of paper onto the floor. Ellen stroked him. A loud, rumbling purr filled the room.

"That's from *The Jungle Books*, isn't it?" I said. "The black panther, Bagheera."

"That's right." Ellen looked at Roddy. "You've read *The Jungle Books*, of course."

Roddy shook his head, for the first time in his life appearing abashed about his nonreading habits.

"You haven't read The Jungle Books?"

"No. I—er—don't read much."

He could have added that he was least likely to read books—including the Kipling classic—that had been pushed on him by parents and teachers.

"Can I stroke him?" Roddy asked. He and the big cat were regarding one another solemnly.

"Not until you know who he is. Bring me that book over there." And she pointed with her other hand. I saw how misshapen it was—more like a gnarled tree branch than a hand.

"What book?" Roddy said, staring in the direction her hand pointed. "There've got to be about a hundred books on that table."

"The red one with the black lettering about three from the top of the second pile."

Then Roddy, my brother Roddy, who never obeyed a command in his life if he could possibly avoid it, went over, took the third book from the second pile and handed it to Ellen.

"Thank you," she said. She opened the book and turned over a few pages. "Now begin there, and read it aloud," she said, handing it back to Roddy. "You may sit on the floor."

When he sat down, a huge amount of dust rose from the carpet. Everybody, including all the cats, sneezed.

"A little dust never hurt anyone," Ellen said. "Read!"

I stood listening to Roddy's cracked voice. " 'It was seven o'clock of a very warm evening in the Seeonee Hills when Father Wolf woke up from his day's rest. . . .' "

I was furious. I must have told my pigheaded little brother a dozen times how much he'd like *The Jungle*

Books because they were all about animals. And his reply, when he bothered to make one, was "Yeah, well, some other time." And there he was, reading the book like a pet lamb, just because that old woman had told him to. I decided to go and inspect the rest of the house.

I went back into the hall, crossed it and went into the room opposite. It was the same size as the room containing the women, but darker and barer, with even more books but few pieces of furniture. Even though it was bright sunlight, the room was dark, because heavy (and, I could see, quite dirty) net curtains hung in front of the panes. Putting my hand out, I touched a switch. A light came on from a chandelier hanging from the center of the ceiling. Dust, gilt and sparkle competed together, and a gentle shower of particles rained down onto the worn, pinkish Persian rug below. Here the books were not only on shelves covering every wall to the ceiling, but also in piles on the floor.

Slowly I walked through the rest of the house's lower story. Behind the room I'd been in was a bedroom, severely modern by contrast. It contained a small, plain cot, a desk, a bureau, one bookcase and a door that probably led to a closet. Behind that was a bathroom with an old-fashioned tub on claw feet, a john with a chain, like some of the older ones in Europe, and framed samplers all over the walls. Behind that was a big square room, empty of furniture except for an easel, a low stand on wheels with paints on top and what looked like an empty crate with the bottom and one side missing. Propped on the easel was an oil painting of what was very likely a black cat, though it could have been a large rat or a small horse. There was a spiral-edged book on top of the crate, probably a book of watercolor paper. From the rippled edges of some of the pages, it appeared as though several had been used.

Here, instead of books, the walls were covered with watercolor paintings, all pinned or taped to the walls. Most of them featured a curious oblong, rigid figure in silver with a red hat, sometimes riding something that was almost certainly a horse and always with either a castle or a forest in the background, occasionally both. In one or two of the drawings were a couple of strange, witchlike figures, holding wands or brooms. There were also one or two drawings featuring a malignant black figure with red eyes, long legs and white teeth. From the shape it could have been either animal or human, but for some reason that I could not pin down, I was sure it was human.

I walked slowly twice around the room to see if there was any sequence or meaning to the paintings as a whole. I had a feeling that there probably was, but that I would have to know what the square or oblong meant to discover it. Ellen's copies of Miranda's paintings were a lot more accurate than the blobby originals. Yet despite the childish, almost irrational qualities of the figures, they had an odd power. I had a feeling they were painted with great passion.

Finally I walked over to the windows. I expected to see an overgrown clearing leading to a circle of undergrowth and trees. Instead there was a high-walled garden. Inside the garden were flowers growing in profusion along the base of the walls and in irregular patches all over the long grass. They were of every color and kind I'd ever seen—not that

I could name more than three of them. Walking among them were more cats and an elderly dachshund.

I went back to the front of the house through a fairly roomy kitchen containing an old range, a gas stove, a sink, some cupboards and a table in the middle. Everything in the kitchen looked ancient, including the paper peeling from the walls, and the ceiling was far too high for the size of the room, giving it the appearance of a deep well.

Through a door in the far side of the kitchen I went back into the living room. Ellen was still working on her graph paper, Miranda was gently feeding the tortoise some of the guinea pig's discarded lettuce and Roddy was sprawled on the sofa with three cats sitting on top of him, one of them being Bagheera.

"How were *The Jungle Books*?" I asked.

"Super. I wish we were staying here instead of with Aunt Chamber Pot."

"Rubbish!" Ellen said briskly. "She may have her faults—in fact, she more than likely does. We all do. But she doesn't deserve to be called that."

"I thought it was rather cute," Roddy said slyly.

"I know you did. But you can't call her—or anyone else—that here. Understand?"

"Yes, okay." Roddy sat up, discomfiting the cats, who seemed to fly in every direction. "Can I come back tomorrow?"

"You can come back anytime, as long as you're not specifically supposed to be somewhere else. But I want your promise that you won't mention my daughter or me or the cats or other animals to a living soul outside. Do I have it?"

"Well, yes, sure," Roddy said. "Why should we—"

"I'm serious about this, Roddy. No one. There is a reason for this which I will not go into now. But it is of the utmost importance. Now tell me that you won't. Because unless I really believe you, you may not come back."

"I promise. Truly. I won't tell a soul. And Betsy won't either, will you, Betsy?"

The woman's dark eyes seemed almost to burn into me.

"No. Of course not," I said.

She looked at me a moment, then nodded. "Good. All right now. You must go."

"Can't we stay a little longer?" Roddy asked. "I can read some more *Jungle Books*."

"I can't think why you haven't read it before," I said crossly. "I've read it, and since all of the nurses-nannies-governesses we've had have been English, I don't see how you escaped. You like animal books."

"Yeah, but I usually find them for myself."

"You didn't find it for yourself this time. Ellen told you to hand it to her, and you did, meek as a lamb."

"Nobody ever told me it was about animals."

"I did," I said combatively.

"Run along, now," Ellen said. "You can have your fight on the way home. You must leave immediately."

"Why?" I asked rudely. "Do you turn into pumpkins?"

"Yes," she said, "large, carnivorous ones, with teeth and black wings. Now go."

"This way." Miranda was holding open the back door.

"Come *on*, Betsy!" Roddy was standing on the porch outside.

The next thing I knew, the door had closed behind us and we were walking back through the woods.

I was furious with Roddy, with those two women, with the cats, with the house and with myself. But most of all with Roddy.

"What got into you?" I said. "I've never seen you like that. You do every blasted thing that old woman suggests, and you can't even be civil to Aunt Marian."

"Aunt Chamber Pot."

"She told you not to say that."

"In *that* house, she said. And anyway, what's it to you? You don't like Aunt Chamber Pot, either."

We walked in angry silence for a while. Just as we reached the beach, Roddy stretched out his hand and took mine. But my feelings were still wounded, so I shook it off.

It was still light when we got back, but it was nearly eight. Aunt Marian and three others were sitting around with drinks and grim expressions.

"Where've you been?" Aunt Marian said.

I stared at her. All I could think about was "Aunt Chamber Pot."

"We took a walk," Roddy said. Since he never spoke to her when he didn't have to, I could see how eager he was to honor his promise to Ellen to keep Aunt Marian well off the scent of the empty house.

"There aren't that many places to walk," Aunt Marian said. "We've been out on the beach looking for you, and then drove into the village to the burger place. We were worried. For a while there wasn't a guard on the beach—despite my telephoning the Club about it." She paused. "*Where* have you been?"

Ellen's imperious old face rose up in front of me, and I could hear her commanding us to tell no one about the empty house or anyone in it. Except, of course, that it wasn't empty.

"We walked along the main road," I said, making it up.

"You walked along the main road, with cars speeding in both directions?" Her voice was a powerful indication of just how insane she thought it was.

"We were going to hitch a ride." Roddy picked up my story.

"To the boardwalk," I finished.

Aunt Marian's brows rose. "That's fifteen miles up the beach."

"That's why we were going to thumb a ride," I said.

"I'm bound to say that shows some initiative." The speaker was a squat, powerful-looking man with shaggy black eyebrows almost covering his eyes. He reminded me of a toad.

"I'm not interested in initiative when I've been worried sick that they might have drowned," Aunt Marian said coldly.

I was staring at the toad when, to my astonishment, he winked at me.

"You told us not to go in when there wasn't a guard, so we didn't, of course." Roddy sounded angelically reasonable. The trouble with his kind of looks is that when he wants to appear like a Norman Rockwell angel, he can—freckles, square face, innocent look and all. I wondered if Aunt Marian would reflect that Roddy had never wasted that kind of look on her before.

Apparently she didn't. "Well, I appreciate that part," she said, obviously soothed. "But I insist, when you take off like that for hours, that you tell me where you're going to go."

"That would take all the fun out of it." Toad of Toad Hall spoke up.

Aunt Marian turned towards him angrily. He got up and waddled to the bar. "Can I give you another drink?" he asked one of the other guests graciously.

"Thanks, Paul. Maybe a small one to keep me going before dinner."

So that was Paul MacTiernan, Aunt Marian's husband. I'd never seen him before.

Aunt Marian glared at him, and drew in her mouth like a tight purse string.

"Well, wash your hands," she said to us. "Dinner will be on in a minute."

"We're going to have to think up a place we can be when we're at the empty house," Roddy said, when we'd excused ourselves after dinner and were walking on the beach. I didn't say anything, because I was torn between agreeing with him and still being jealous at his unquestioning acceptance of Ellen and Miranda.

"Why do you like them so much?" I asked.

It was a silly question, and I knew it the minute I asked. Furthermore, I didn't think his reply would answer the question I was really asking. I wasn't even sure what that question was.

"Because . . . because they're *real*—not like Aunt Potty."

"They're slightly nuts, you know that, don't you? Especially Miranda."

"Yeah. I know that. I still think they're more real."

I didn't say anything for a while. Roddy had answered the essential question. "Yes. I guess you're right," I said finally. Then I added, "Uncle Paul winked at me."

"He doesn't look too bad. Fat—but not bad." We walked a few paces. It was almost dark. "There's Ted and Tiger," Roddy said, and ran to meet them.

I walked slowly towards Ted, who was watching Roddy and Tiger chase each other around.

"Tiger's really found a friend," Ted said.

"Roddy calls him Superdog."

Ted grinned. "Quite accurate. That's just what he is."

"Do you have any more pets, at home, I mean?"

"I had a dog, but he died this spring. Lived to be sixteen, so I can't complain, but I sure miss him. And then we have a couple of cats, and my kid brother has a rabbit."

Without saying anything, I had joined Ted and we had turned and were walking back the way he had come—in the direction of the village.

"Well, now you have Tiger to take his place."

"That's what I was thinking, if Tiger and I can just stay out of trouble around the burger joint." We walked a bit. Then Ted asked, "Is it just you and Roddy? Any more siblings?"

"No. Just Roddy and me."

"You seem close. I mean, closer than a lot of brothers and sisters are. Is it because you've lived abroad?"

"A little. We've moved around a lot. And then there's . . . the divorce. That makes a difference." It was hard explaining my feeling for Roddy without going into Daddy's being in jail, or Roddy's illness. "He's very independent," I said finally. "But well . . . I guess it's because we're here alone."

We walked along in silence. I felt I had sounded stupid, which upset me quite a lot. I didn't want to sound stupid in front of Ted.

"I know I sound, well . . . not very bright."

Ted reached out and took my hand. Without even thinking, I found myself squeezing his.

"You don't sound anything but intelligent and nice," Ted said. He turned, and in the moonlight I could see him smile. There was a queer, jumpy feeling inside that had never happened to me before. His hand was warm and strong and a little sandy.

"Your hand is sandy," I said.

"Sorry." He unclasped my hand and let it go.

"No, I didn't mean that," I said, feeling idiotic. "I *like* it that way, warm and strong and sandy."

He'd taken my hand again. And each of us was squeezing the other's hand now. "Good." His voice had a breathy quality. "I feel that way about yours. That I like it."

The way his head was tilted put his mouth in shadow. I found myself wondering how it would feel against mine. If it would be sandy . . . and then I could feel myself blushing all over. I'd never had thoughts like that about anybody.

Ted was looking down at me, but suddenly looked over my shoulder.

"Roddy seems to be taking Tiger for a swim. Is that okay with you?"

I spun around. I couldn't tell whether Roddy was actually in the water or merely at the water's edge. Then I saw that he was in, and that the water came up almost to the top of his jeans legs. And Tiger seemed to be swimming out.

"Call Tiger, Ted, would you?" I said. "I don't want Roddy going out like that alone."

Ted put his hands up to his mouth and gave a piercing whistle. I saw both Roddy and Tiger turn. Roddy started wading for the shore, but Tiger beat him. He paused at the water's edge, shook himself and then tore after us.

"Good boy, good boy," Ted said, patting him.

Roddy was slowly moving in our direction. He paused then, and seemed to stand stock still for a second, on the verge of taking another step.

I froze, convinced he was going to have a seizure. But after a minute, he leaned down, picked up something on the sand and continued towards us.

"Is Roddy okay?" Ted asked.

"He has . . . he has an illness," I said.

"I thought there might be something," Ted said.

I stared at him. "What made you think that?"

"Just something about the two of you together. As though you had a secret."

"We have more than one," I said grimly. "Ted, please don't tell anyone, including Roddy, what I told you."

"Of course not." He glanced down at me. "You can trust me."

"I know," I said, and the jumpy feeling inside my chest had come back. "I know I can."

"What've you got there, Roddy?" Ted asked.

"Some kind of a shell." Roddy was looking at the curly shell. "I like shells."

"You can get quite a variety here after high tide."

"Roddy," I said, "I hate to sound fussy, but you're soaked."

"Yeah, I know, and if I run into Aunt Potty she'll make a big thing of it."

"Go in the back way. Maybe Cinda will hang your jeans up to dry, or put 'em in the dryer."

"Okay. 'Bye, Tiger. 'Bye, Ted."

"Who's Aunt Potty?" Ted asked. He glanced at me and I could see him grin. "Mrs. MacTiernan?"

I giggled. "Yes. Roddy doesn't like her."

"Can't say I blame him." He paused. "I guess I better get back. See you soon."

I watched him walking along the beach and realized that he had come here specially to see me. It made me feel wonderful.

For a while I sat on the sand and stared at the ocean and the night sky. There was a big moon, not full yet, but lopsided. It was hard to realize that it was a place people had trod on. Once Father had said, "If we can manage not to blow ourselves up, there's no place in the universe that, eventually, we can't go—if not in body, at least in consciousness."

"What do you mean by that?" I asked.

"I mean it's all One, capital-O One."

"What is?"

"God, you, me, the universe, that squirrel over there—the whole shooting match."

"I thought you were brought up a Catholic."

He sighed. "I was. But being a Catholic is not—despite what your mother and aunt think—an impediment to rational thinking."

"I don't think I know what you're talking about."

"That's all right. It'll come to you."

That was one of the things I liked about Father. He never believed that everything had to be explained in terms suitable for a ten-year-old.

"Hello," a voice said beside me. "Mind if I sit down? That is, if I can manage it?"

I looked up. It was Toad. "Hello, Uncle Paul. Do sit down. Did you wink at me?"

"Yes, I did. Did you mind?"

"No, I thought it was fun."

"I thought you might. That's why I did it." There

was a great deal of panting and groaning, and then he sat down beside me. "The one thing every right-thinking person is united about," he said, still puffing, "is that I should lose weight."

I knew instantly that it was the kind of thing Aunt Marian would think. "If you don't want to, I don't see why you should. It's your body."

"You see, I was right. You are a kindred soul. I knew it anyway, because although you have all those elegant bones from your mother's family, you have your father's hands and manner."

"I didn't know you knew him. I mean, after all, I've never seen you before."

"No, you and I haven't met, which is definitely my loss. But I knew your father when he and your mother were first married, and we have had lunches together in the city sometimes when he was in New York on business trips. I've always liked him very much."

All of a sudden I was crying. A lot of people had said a lot of things when he was indicted—how sorry they were, and how difficult it must be for his family, and how much they sympathized with him and what could they do? But this was the first time that somebody had said, simply, that he liked him.

I groped around in my pocket for a handkerchief.

"Here," Uncle Paul said. And he gave me a handful of clean tissues. I took them and cried and blew and wiped and then cried and blew and wiped some more. "Thanks," I said. "I mean, not just for the tissues. But for what you said. Father's innocent. I mean, he didn't know that creep was stealing the money."

Uncle Paul said slowly, "I'd certainly like to believe it. But you know, he did plead guilty. And technically, of course, he was. It was his company. And the accountant said he was following orders—orders from your father."

"But he wasn't. I'm sure he wasn't. Because Father's not like that. But they all believed the accountant. It's crazy!"

"I will say, the whole thing, the investigation, the arrest and indictment and the trial, happened awfully fast. I've rarely seen the law move with so much dispatch."

"I just wish there were something I could do."

"I'm not sure now if anything can be done. When the whole thing hit the papers I, too, wondered about the accountant. I even went so far as to make some inquiries of my own. But that young man seems to have lived a blameless life since he was out of the playpen. Which turned me off."

"Why did it put you off?" For some reason I found that statement hopeful.

"I don't know. Probably sheer cussedness. I've always found that much virtue in one human being debilitating. But please don't quote me."

"I won't," I said, and grinned at him.

"And now," Uncle Paul said, "I'm contemplating a much more difficult feat than anything else we discussed."

"What's that?"

"Getting up. How strong's your shoulder?"

Chapter Five

It was the next morning that something made me pick up the vial containing Roddy's medicine to see how many pills were left. When I saw there were none, I could feel a cold pang in my stomach.

When Roddy was seven, he fell off his bicycle and hit his head on the hard street. There didn't seem to be any lasting damage. And then, six months later, he had a convulsion. Unfortunately, it happened at school, and the wrong man was in charge of the class at the time. His prescription for getting Roddy over the pain and embarrassment of the episode was to joke him out of it, a tactic joyfully embraced by Roddy's classmates, who gave him more of the same treatment when he had two seizures the following week. When Father, who had been away, discovered what had happened, he stalked into the school and removed Roddy, but not before telling the teacher and the boys exactly what he thought of them.

After several days in the hospital for Roddy, and a variety of tests, the doctors gave Father and Mother their diagnosis: epilepsy. Roddy was put on anticonvulsive medicine that seemed to work well. He had no more seizures. And my father made sure that the new school where Roddy was sent, and the schoolmasters, were properly forewarned. Even so, Roddy never again felt completely at ease, completely trusting, among his peers. Once or twice when we had to board at school, he took great care to hide his medicine. I found out about that when he wanted a small box with a lock that he could take back to school after Christmas.

"What've you got that's so private?" I asked kiddingly.

"My medicine."

"Roddy, people don't care." It was a useless thing to say, and I knew it. Roddy cared. But I persisted. "They probably don't know, and if they did, it wouldn't strike them as anything peculiar. After all, people take medicines for things all the time."

"Yeah? When I was walking down the front hall one day, on my way to the dorm, I heard one of the boys in my class say to a new boy, 'See that kid with red hair? The American? He has fits.' They bloody well do know."

All of this slid through my mind as I picked the empty container out of the back of the medicine cabinet. Simply seeing the vial there should have warned me. If it had been full, it would have been hidden in his underwear drawer.

I knocked and then went into his room.

"Roddy—"

"I didn't say 'Come in,' " Roddy said, pulling on his T-shirt. "You don't have any right to open the door till I say it's okay."

"Sorry. I was upset. Why didn't you tell me you'd run out of your medicine?"

"Because I don't need it anymore."

"Roddy! You can't know that. You can't be sure. And you can't risk—"

"I haven't had . . . I haven't . . . I haven't been ill for at least a year and a half. You know the doctor said I'd probably grow out of it. Well, he was right. I have. I can feel it."

"You don't want to take that risk. I mean—think!"

"I don't have to think. I know. I've been there, remember? You haven't. And I know it's gone."

The more I talked, the more mulish-looking he got. He wanted so passionately to be rid of the albatross that he had arrived, illogically, at the conviction that if he could just stop taking that daily reminder, the medicine, then the illness itself would go away.

"Roddy, it doesn't work that way. It's the medicine that keeps . . . keeps the symptoms from happening."

"The doctor said I'd grow out of it."

"He said you might. Maybe. But not absolutely definitely. I thought Mother told you to get a whole year's supply before we came over here. Where's the rest?''

There was a slight pause, then, "In my suitcase."

If there hadn't been that pause, I would have believed him. But Roddy doesn't lie well—at least not to me.

"That's not true, is it? You don't have any more. Roddy . . ." I reached out and took his arm.

He shook it off. "I'm going to get some breakfast."

He started down the hall. I called after him, "I'm going to have to ask Aunt Marian to suggest a doctor who can prescribe some more of your pills."

He'd been almost at the stairs, but he turned back. His face was white and his freckles like brown spots. "If you tell Aunt Potty, Betsy, I'll never speak to you again. I mean it!" And he went downstairs. I followed slowly.

As I drank my coffee and nibbled at a piece of toast, I pondered what I could do. The choices seemed to be, on the one hand, to tell Aunt Marian, which would serve Roddy right for being so pigheaded. But I knew why he hated the idea. Aunt Marian was an untrustworthy adult who might start discussing "Roddy's weakness" or "Roddy's ailment" in a certain kind of voice that would ensure that sooner or later, and probably sooner, everybody on the beach would know about it. Certainly her friends would know, which would mean their children, which could mean . . . As though on a movie screen in my head, I could see Roddy striding out onto the beach amid a battery of knowing looks, walking with what seemed to everybody else to be a swagger of confidence, but which I knew was an act of defiance in the face of the gods. . . . Aunt Marian must not know.

On the other hand, I felt responsible for seeing to it that Roddy got a refill of his medicine. If he didn't, and if he had another seizure, it would be my fault, no matter what anybody said.

"You're very quiet," Aunt Marian said. "You okay?" She sounded almost human.

"Fine," I said.

"What are the two of you planning to do today? I'd take you to the Club, but I have an appointment this morning, and I won't be going in that direction."

"Swim," I said, not having the faintest intention of doing so.

"Take a walk," Roddy chimed in.

"But not to the boardwalk," Aunt Marian said. "Why don't you just go onto the beach. There are always kids there playing games of one kind or another. And I've already checked. There's a guard on duty."

"Okay," Roddy said, folding his angelic wings and looking good enough to eat. I knew exactly what he was planning.

Evidently Aunt Marian was not as stupid as I'd given her credit for. She stared fixedly at Roddy for a moment before she returned her attention to the local newspaper. "I don't know why I bother to read this nonsense," she said. "It's filled with nothing but society gossip."

"You love society gossip," Uncle Paul said from across the table. A neat pile of rather drab-looking toast was beside his plate. The plate in front of him was full of flaky-looking crumbs. Aunt Marian looked over her half reading glasses. "You haven't eaten any of your protein bread," she said to her husband.

"Oh yes I did," Uncle Paul said. "You just didn't notice."

Aunt Marian glared at him. "Then what are croissant crumbs doing in your plate?"

"I can't imagine. They must have jumped over from your plate." Uncle Paul heaved himself to his feet. "Anybody want a lift? Walter's taking me to the train."

I stood up. "I'll have a lift, thank you, Uncle Paul."

"I knew I'd strike it lucky sooner or later," Uncle Paul said.

Aunt Marian was looking at the rejected protein bread. "I don't know why you defy me like this," she said sorrowfully. "It's not *my* overweight, or *my* cholesterol, or *my* heart."

"No," Uncle Paul said, waddling over, "and it's a great consolation to me that you're thin and healthy." He kissed her cheek.

"Thanks a lot. What kind of consolation do you

think it is for me to know you're a walking heart attack?"

"Are you really a walking heart attack?" I asked Uncle Paul when we were in the car.

"Yes. Your aunt's quite right. I should do exactly what she says I should do." He sighed. "And what my doctor says."

"Then why don't you?"

"Because I don't like to be ganged up on. If that sounds infantile, then I'm willing to admit to that, too."

A newspaper had once referred to Uncle Paul as a "captain of industry." My father said that Uncle Paul had one of the best business minds he'd ever come across. The image of the captain of industry with his fine business mind behaving like a child of three who wouldn't eat his porridge was too much. I giggled. "You're like Roddy," I said.

He looked over at me and smiled. "Where do you want me to drop you?"

"At the drugstore," I said. I had no particular reason to go to the drugstore, but I had accepted Uncle Paul's offer of a lift simply to get away and think. Also, I realized, because I debated consulting him. But he was Aunt Marian's husband. He might feel he had to tell her. "There were a couple of things I forgot to bring," I finished off.

"The drugstore it is."

After the car drove off, I stood on the sidewalk in front of the small shopping mall and tried to think. The various stores of the village took up three sides of the shopping mall. The fourth side was open to the ocean. The burger shop was at the end of one of the sides, and I realized that in the back of my mind all along was the thought of talking to Ted.

As I allowed myself to think his name, I could feel my heart give a little jump. Underneath everything else last night, while I was talking to Uncle Paul and when I was lying in bed, staring up at the ceiling, waiting to go to sleep, was the thought of our time together on the beach. I could feel again the slight brush of sand on his hand and his warm, strong fingers around mine. Did he feel the same way about me? And wasn't it odd that I should fall in love with a rangy boy who wore glasses and wasn't really handsome—not the way Larry Babcock was handsome. Then—"Stop!" I said to myself. "Whoa—slow down!" I could feel my heart galloping.

I glanced at my watch. It was eight-fifteen. Would the shop be open, and if it were, would Ted be there? There was only one way to find out.

The shop was open and Ted was there.

Ted had his back to me, serving someone on the far side of the counter, as I slid onto a stool. Then he turned and saw me, and we both smiled. I knew then that I hadn't imagined it all, and that he did feel the same way as I did.

"Hi," he said, and came over. "Breakfast at home not up to scratch?"

I started to blush, and could feel it going all the way down my neck and shoulders and up my face. Until he said that, it hadn't occurred to me how it might look for me to come and see Ted practically at the crack of dawn: as though I were chasing him.

"Hey!" he said. "Joke! I'm glad to see you. I hope all your breakfasts are terrible." And he put some coffee down in front of me. "Will that do for a start?"

"Fine. Thanks."

The restaurant was pretty empty, and those cus-
tomers who were there looked like business types.
Two men, each reading a paper, were sitting at the
other end of the counter.

"Ted. There's something I want to talk to you
about."

"Sure," he said. "Let me just give these two guys
their checks."

I watched him as he quickly scribbled on the small
pad from his pocket, put the checks down beside the
men and made change for them at the cash register.
All over again, I thought what a nice smile he had.
His face, under the thick, light-brown hair, was
tanned, and his smile white by contrast. He
managed, I thought, to look both highly intelligent
and sexy. And the men seemed to like him, talking
to him as though he were another man, not a boy.

"Okay," he said, coming back. "What can I do?"

"What I'm about to tell you," I said, "you won't
repeat, ever, please."

The gray eyes behind the glasses were level and
very mature. "Not if you ask me not to." I knew I
could trust him.

I took a breath. "Thanks. It's not about me, it's about Roddy." And I told him about Roddy's illness and the problem about the medicine. "If I tell Aunt Marian, I'm afraid she'll make a big to-do, and even mention it to some of her friends. I know that sounds as though I think she's some kind of a fink, but I just don't see her understanding how Roddy feels. And if any of the mothers know, then the kids will know. And sooner or later somebody will say something. That's happened before. It's been rough on him. But he's got to take the medicine until a doctor tells him it's all right not to."

"Can't your parents send some more?"

"No." It was the moment I could say, "My father's in prison." But I didn't say it, and the moment passed.

"The pills were prescribed in England, where we lived until recently. And my father—he can't be reached right now. They're divorced." Again, I hadn't said the magic words, "My father's in prison," and part of me jeered at me for being a coward and a traitor. "Mother's in England, married again, except that right now she isn't there. She works for a magazine and is on assignment."

Ted pushed the white cap he wore to the back of his head. "That's a tough one. How about me scrambling you some eggs while I'm thinking about it."

"I've had breakfast."

"Oh."

"Officially, that is. All I ate was a piece of toast."

"Eggs coming up," he said.

In a minute he had them in front of me, with a toasted muffin beside them. "You know, Betsy, there are not a lot of choices. Even if the same medicine, in the same strength, went by the same brand name over here, you'd have to have a doctor's prescription to get it, and no doctor worth his salt is going to give it to you without examining Roddy. Your best bet would be to call the English doctor, or maybe the English drugstore, and get them to send over a supply. Even then it would take several days, unless there's some kind of overnight service, which would probably cost the earth."

Having had no appetite for breakfast at the beach

house, I found I was wolfing down Ted's eggs and muffin with great enthusiasm. "You shake a mean pan," I said. "These eggs are delicious."

He grinned. "I'll make some girl a nice husband."

I blushed again. I could feel the heat in my face, which embarrassed me and, of course, made me blush more.

He said, "You look nice when you blush."

The heat surged back. I couldn't help it. I giggled. He grinned.

"How's Tiger?" I said.

"I gave him a huge breakfast and took him over to spend the day with some friends. At least he won't be lonely." He glanced up as two more people came in and sat at the counter. "Be back," he said.

I finished my breakfast and pondered Ted's comments about Roddy's medicine. What he had said was true. Either I had to get Roddy to go to a local doctor who could prescribe the American equivalent of what he'd been taking, or I had to telephone England. But that would involve using Aunt Marian's phone, and if I were to do that, I might as well go ahead and talk to her. Of course, I could use a phone booth and be armed with plenty of change. I tried to keep my mind on Roddy's problem, but it kept being distracted by the way Ted's muscle curved as it emerged from his rolled-up sleeve. Stop being a fatuous idiot, I told myself, but kept right on watching him.

"On second, third and fourth thoughts," Ted said, coming back with a second cup of coffee for me, "I think the best solution is to phone England. Didn't you say your mother lives there?"

"Yes, she works for a news magazine there. It's an American magazine, but she works out of the London bureau. And right now she's going around Europe finding out what people think about the Common Market. It's all because there's some kind of election about to take place in England."

"My father's a journalist, or at least a reporter, and I'm a stringer here—"

"Hey, Ted! I'm starved. How about some breakfast?" Another man, who had just come in and sat down, was trying to sound funny, but only managed to sound annoyed. "Not that I want to interfere in your social life."

"You couldn't," Ted said evenly. "What'll you have? I'll be back," he muttered to me as he went to take the man's order.

One of the things—one of the several things—I liked about Ted was the way nobody was able to put him down. He managed to keep his end up without blowing up or getting mad. I watched him take down a box of cereal from the shelf, pour some milk and put two slices of toast into the toaster. I dragged my mind back to Roddy and his problem. The best thing to do, I decided, was to try and call from a phone booth. The best of all things, I decided, would be to talk to his doctor. Even so, that meant that Roddy would be without the medicine for at least another four or five days.

"Where's a good phone booth?" I asked when Ted came back.

"For a transatlantic call?" He stared out the window behind my back. "Most of the phone booths are just that—glass booths in the middle of nowhere, and there's usually a line of three or four kids waiting outside, or even crowded together inside."

"Don't they have phones at home? I thought everybody in America had phones."

Ted looked at me with his half smile. "There are times when you sound like a foreigner."

"Most of the time I feel like one—everywhere."

He reached out and took my hand, which was resting on the counter. "You're not," he said.

Once again my heart seemed to jump and it was suddenly hard to breathe.

"How old are you?" he asked.

"Almost sixteen. How old are you?"

"Seventeen."

"Any service around here?" an irritated voice said.

"Be back," he muttered, releasing my hand, and went over to wait on a new customer who'd sat down at the counter. I could feel the blood coming up in my cheeks again, and cursed my blushability.

"He just wanted coffee," Ted said, coming back. "I've been thinking. There's a motel outside the village, on the main road. It's not too far, less than a quarter of a mile. Anyway, they have whole rows of public telephones in their lobby. You'd probably get the greatest privacy there. You'd better call pretty soon. It's a five-hour difference."

I'd forgotten all about it, which was pretty silly, since I was the one who had lived abroad. "Yes. It'd be"—I looked at the clock on the wall—"about one-thirty now. Maybe I ought to wait for an hour, make sure everybody's back from lunch."

Ted scribbled on a check and put it beside me. "Sorry to charge you, but the boss would fire me if he thought I was giving free meals to my friends."

I stared at the check and felt the hated, humiliating heat surge up again in my face. My money was in my little shoulder bag back at the beach house. I didn't have so much as a quarter with me.

"Ted," I said, miserably, "I'm sorry. I got a lift from Uncle Paul and forgot all about my bag. I'll go home and get it."

"Tsk-tsk," Ted said, taking the check back and tearing it up. "Forget it."

"Is there any hope of getting any service around here?" the same irritated voice asked.

"I'll call you," Ted said.

Just as I left, I saw the manager come bounding out of his office. The kindest thing I could do for Ted, I thought, was split—immediately.

I went back to the beach house as fast as I could, running and walking and thinking and mentally kicking myself for being so stupid as to show up at the burger shop with no money. What would Ted think? He'd think exactly what I was afraid he would think: that I was chasing after him and being pushy; that this whole business about Roddy was just an excuse to see him. That made me so miserable that I ran even faster.

There was no one in the house when I returned. A note from Aunt Marian was lying in the middle of the floor, pinned down with a paperweight.

Betsy and/or Roddy:
    Have gone out and will have lunch at the Club. If Cinda is out shopping, please leave her a note to say whether you (one or both) will be back for lunch. Remember, dinner at eight, promptly.

I was so relieved to be in the house alone that I almost did a dance. I went upstairs, put all my regular money in my jeans pocket, checked to make sure the envelope containing the five thousand was still taped to the underside of the bureau drawer and scribbled a note for Cinda.

"Roddy and I will be out to lunch. Betsy."

I couldn't be absolutely certain about Roddy, but something told me that he was at the empty house and had every intention of staying there for the rest of the day. Sooner or later I would have to go and collect him, I knew. For the first time, Ellen's statement—no telephone—hit me. The only way to reach Roddy was to go there.

Then I jogged back to the burger shop. The round trip had taken me a little less than an hour.

The moment I walked into the shop, I knew that something had happened. The manager was walking around looking vaguely unpleasant, and there were a lot of people clustered at the counter. Ted glanced at me, smiled, made a slight gesture with his hand

and then went on serving without looking at me again.

Once more I could feel that awful blush rush into my face. I was now certain that Ted, the manager and a few other assorted types around the burger shop were sure I was chasing him. I walked up to the counter and held out a five-dollar bill.

"I'm sorry I forgot to bring money the last time," I said, very formally. "Thanks for letting me go back and get it."

Ted had turned to me. For one brief second his eyes went to the manager. Then he took the five-dollar bill. "Thanks," he said, and went to the cash register. When he brought back the change, he said to me, "By the way, I wrote down the name and telephone number of a doctor here. He's supposed to be good." Ted took a folded slip of paper out of his breast pocket. "If you can't connect with the doctor overseas, you could talk to this one."

"Thanks, Ted. Thanks a lot."

"I'll call you."

"Ted!" somebody yelled. "There's more than one customer, you know!"

"Not for me," Ted said under his breath, and grinned.

I left feeling as though I were walking on air.

And as I headed towards the motel to make the call to London, I continued to float happily. I'd read about falling in love, but it had always seemed remote—something that happened to other people. I'd never been able even to imagine it, and now I couldn't imagine *not* being in love. It was like a miracle that couldn't unhappen, and I felt bathed in a kind of happy idiocy.

After a while, though, as I got nearer the motel, reality pushed its way into my consciousness. Reality meant, first and foremost, Father, locked in a prison not too many miles away. I had found out that I could go and see him, but, being under sixteen, I would have to be accompanied by an adult. Until now, the only possible adults were Aunt Marian and the lawyer, who, I thought, had done nothing for Father. He had just sat there and let my father get pushed into prison by that horrible judge, who seemed to decide everything in favor of the prosecution. I thought lawyers were supposed to get people out of trouble, to prevent them from going to jail.

To ask Aunt Marian to take me to see Father was more than I could bear. I was quite sure that she'd be long-suffering about it—that is, if she agreed to do it at all. But now I'd met Uncle Paul. As soon as he got back this evening I'd ask him, though even he said it would be hard to get my father's name and reputation restored.

My spirits fell.

Then there was Roddy and his medicine and his hiding out at the empty house. I didn't blame him for preferring Ellen and Miranda and the animals to the beach and the kids. But the doctor had once said to Roddy, "You know, you're going to have to come out of hiding. You're going to have to learn to live with this. The chances are it won't give you any more trouble. But even so, you must come out and take the risk."

"That's pretty easy to say," Roddy had replied. His green eyes had blazed with anger. "You don't have the problem."

"How do you know? Lots of people you pass in the street, living their lives, have the problem."

I found out from the overseas operator that the call would cost over ten dollars. "May I have ten dollars in quarters, please," I said to the man behind the motel desk. The plaque said he was an assistant manager.

He gave me a cold look. "Are you staying here?"

"No."

"Then I'm sorry. We can't give out that many quarters. We may need them."

"But I have to make an overseas telephone call. To a doctor," I finished, as the man looked increasingly unsympathetic.

"Aren't the doctors here good enough for you?" He was the kind of man who was smooth all over, smooth face, smooth hair, smooth suit, smooth eyes.

"I think that's a stupid comment. There's a gas station next door, I'll go and get them there."

"In that case you can use the phone booth across the street."

"Why are you being so nasty? These are public

phones here, and I have a right to use one of them. And I'd bet the telephone company would agree with me."

"Since they own all the phones, it doesn't matter to them which phone you use. But it does to us. We're tired of having you kids come into the motel, sprawl all over the lobby and use our phones."

"What's the trouble?" a familiar voice said behind me.

The man looked over my shoulder. "Oh, hello, Ted. This girl wants me to give her forty quarters so she can spend all day on our phones." The manner and words were just as hostile, but the man looked a little less sure of himself.

"I do not," I said. "I told you, I want to call our doctor in England."

"She's telling the truth," Ted joined in. Her br—" He glanced at me and corrected himself. "A member of her family is ill and she has to discuss with the doctor his sending the medicine they've been using."

The man sighed and opened a drawer under the counter. "We know you, Ted, and we know your father. So—here's the forty quarters." And he placed the roll on the desk.

I handed over the ten-dollar bill. "Thanks," I said, as nastily as I knew how. But my heart was doing a funny tattoo, because Ted was standing there, sticking up for me, helping me.

"Let's go. I'll stand outside the booth so nobody will bother you," he said.

"Listen," I said. "I'm sorry if I made trouble for you at the burger place."

"It's okay. It wasn't you. It was that creep of a customer. Even after you left and I gave him my undivided attention, he complained. Then he told the manager about my tearing up your check, and everything hit the fan. The manager usually stops just short of firing me because other people he's tried out behind the counter haven't been any good, but the air was a little thick when you walked in. But when he saw who it was that I'd given credit to, he calmed right down and said that anytime I wanted to extend credit to you, it would be all right. He's nothing if not a snob about the richer families in the area."

"That's not fair," I said.

"No, but it's reality. His store has to make at least three quarters of its annual income during the summer months, and it makes it from the children of people like the MacTiernans. Here's your booth."

I slid in, deposited a dime, and asked for the overseas operator. Luckily, at the last moment, I decided to make the call to the doctor person to person. It would have been much more expensive if he'd been in, but he was in Italy on vacation, and his regular nurse also seemed to be on holiday. There was another doctor on call, but he was not available at the moment, and anyway, I thought, he didn't know Roddy. For the moment, that seemed to be that. I did reach the drugstore. But it was a large establishment, and the pharmacist had no memory of either Roddy or me and without the doctor's personal approval, he flatly refused to send the medicine overseas.

"Much better to go to a doctor where you are," the druggist finished. "After all, at this point, he might need a different dosage."

"Thanks a lot," I said.

I sat staring at the phone after I'd hung up. Outside, Ted was looking over the newspaper and magazine rack. Suddenly a memory, something I had paid no attention to at the time, slid into my mind: Ted had said his father was a reporter.

Until my father had been indicted, reporters and journalists were good guys. After all, Mother was a working journalist, although she wrote more on things like the economic decline of the dollar or the pound, or the changing aspects of European socialism than (to quote my father) who murdered whom at the corner bar.

But since Father's indictment, reporters had been at the bottom of the heap as far as I was concerned: miserable, lying, distorting, deliberately perverting purveyors of misinformation for the public's misunderstanding. (I was quoting one of my father's few supporters, but I couldn't remember who.) They talked about my father as though he was some greedy multinational head oppressing the poor employee. One or two of the columnists interviewed at length all the employees who felt that Father had left them with the debt to the U.S. government still to pay, and did not bother to interview other employees who still believed in him.

Two or three of the latter did get their protesting letters printed in the letters columns. But the small print could hardly match in power the column headline: "Wealthy corporation president tries to cheat on employees' tax." I think that hurt Father most of all. As a working man himself, he had identified very much with his own employees.

I found myself wishing violently that Ted's father would be of the "future of the franc" type of journalist, writing essays on economic trends. But I was afraid it wasn't so.

Thinking of Mother made me decide to try and reach her. After I managed to get more change from the assistant manager a long (and expensive) phone call to her office in London told me what I feared: She was somewhere on her journey, collecting information on the Common Market and how it was viewed by the continental Europeans.

"The best we can do," the pleasant girl in Mother's London office said, "is to give her the message to call you whenever she calls in."

"All right," I replied. And hung up.

Outside, Ted was still reading his newspaper. I sat there, filled with a dull anger against Mother. Why wasn't she here when Roddy and I needed her?

The answer to that was perfectly simple: She had remarried and had her own home in England. But right now I wanted someone else to have to make the choice about Roddy's medicine. Someone else— but not Aunt Marian.

Ted looked up, saw me sitting in the booth, staring, and smiled at me.

I opened the booth door.

"Get anybody?" he asked.

"No. The doctor's on holiday, the druggist won't send it without the doctor's approval, and Mother's off in Germany somewhere."

"When will the doctor be back?"

"In a couple of weeks, his secretary said."

"Can it wait that long?"

"I don't know. Roddy says the doctor in England did say he was going to phase Roddy off his medicine."

"Have you tried the doctor here?"

"No. Not yet. You see, even if I made an appointment, I'm not sure how I can force Roddy to go, and do the whole thing without Aunt Marian's knowing. Because, as you said, no good doctor would give him medicine without all sorts of tests, the kind you usually have to have in a hospital."

"Well . . ." Ted said. "You may be right. But he might have a solution. Give him a ring."

"I will," I said. But I didn't move, because I was looking at the newspaper Ted had hanging from his hand as he leaned against the back of a leather sofa and talked. The paper was upside down, but the masthead was easy to make out. I recognized the paper immediately. It was not one of the great newspapers but one serving a town near which Father had one of his plants. Nevertheless, it had its own reputation, and its leading columnist-reporter had been one of Father's chief attackers.

"Why are you reading that paper in particular?" I asked, with a terrible foreboding.

"Dad works for it. I usually wait until I get home

to read his column, or I get it before I go to work. But I thought I might as well read it while you were phoning. Why?"

"Is your last name Lockwood?"

"That's right."

I stared at Ted, with his intelligent face, nice smile and handsome body. The most terrific boy I'd ever met. The boy I was in love with.

"What's wrong, Betsy?"

"What's wrong is that your father did his best to destroy mine."

Chapter Six

We stared at each other, the tension between us drawn tight.

Then, "What are you talking about?" Ted said. And before I could answer, "Who are you?"

"My father is Geoffrey Smith. One of the things your father called him was 'an archetype of the corporate criminal.' He also said that three years was 'a mere slap on the wrist.' " The brutal sentences poured out of me as though I had learned them by heart, and as though it were happening all over again. "He said he hoped 'Geoffrey Smith's family would learn what it was like to be poor and in trouble.' He said . . ."

But that was as far as I got. My voice gave out. I groped in my jeans for a tissue. "He's a horrible, stupid, malicious, lying man. I know he's your father, but he had no right to say that. . . . It's not true." I gave up trying not to cry, and cried.

After a minute, Ted said, "He's none of those things." And then, "My God! What a mess!"

After another while, he said, "Do you want me to go away?"

I'd been quite sure I did, but found myself shaking my head. "No."

"We're going to have to talk about this," Ted said slowly. "I have to go back to the burger shop now. What about this evening?"

I nodded. "What time?"

"Seven?"

"Okay."

We looked at each other gravely. Then Ted

said, "I'll see you then," and walked out of the motel.

For a long time I sat in the leather chair in the motel lobby. At first I kept thinking about Ted, trying to put into the same frame the way I felt about him and the hatred I felt for his father. As though they were tapes playing in my head, I heard again everything Max Lockwood had written, plus all the other articles, just as bad and sometimes worse, written by other newsmen, and the fact that everything—the stories, the quotes, the interviews— seemed to be designed to make my father look bad.

The assistant manager passed, and stopped. "Got your call in?"

"Yes thanks." There didn't seem any point in telling him that nobody was home.

"That's a real nice kid, that Ted Lockwood. Reminds me of his old man—works hard and is always for the little guy."

"Ted's always for the little guy? What do you mean?"

"Well, I guess I was talking about Max, his father. But Ted's a reporter, too. He has some kind of free-lance arrangement with one of the local papers. A stringer, I guess you'd call him. If he sends them an item and they use it, he gets paid."

I remembered then Ted's words in the burger place, about being a stringer. Only I was so bewitched over Ted himself that the words hadn't registered.

"Sorry I wasn't very cooperative at first," the assistant manager said. "I didn't know you were a friend of the Lockwoods'. But a lot of the kids come here and hang around the lobby, playing with the video games we have outside the bar, and also trying to order drinks. It's a headache, because most of them are underage, but they get fake identification from somewhere, and then some parent gets in an uproar and we have the police on our hands."

Avoiding the mall, I went straight to the beach and began the long walk to the empty house. I had to have a talk with Roddy about his medicine. Along with everything else, I was furious with him for being such an ostrich. It was his illness, not mine. If he would just *help,* we could figure out what to do. But then I remembered his face when he came home from school one day. The schoolmaster—the one who believed in the kidding approach—had been particularly funny on the subject of people who had fits. . . . Roddy didn't cry. He clenched his teeth and stood his ground. But something in his eyes—an anguished amalgam of pride and pain—showed the cost. Pretending now that the whole thing had just gone away was, I supposed, one way of dealing with it.

It was strange, I thought, standing in front of the house again, how empty it looked. I realized now that the heavy, dirty net curtains somehow added to the abandoned look. Even in the back living room, the room where they spent most of the time—or at least Ellen did, with her canvases and pieces of wool—the net material, helpfully incrusted with dust, acted as a shield from any eyes that might look in. But whoever did now, except, on freak occasions, people like us?

Miranda opened the back door, and the powerful animal odor hit me in the face once more. I was astonished to see that she wasn't in the wheelchair.

"I thought you couldn't walk," I said.

"I never told you that. So don't pretend I did. If I feel like being in a wheelchair, I'll be in a wheel-chair. If I don't, then I don't." She almost slammed the door behind me and walked in a queer, pigeon-toed way towards the front of the house. Dangling from one hand was a paintbrush.

Ellen was in the living room, her head bent over her lap board, coloring the canvas resting on the board. Roddy was sitting cross-legged on the floor, reading aloud while with one hand he fed some carrot to Sebastian. He looked up as I came in. "Hi," he said, and went back to the adventures of Rikki-tikki-tavi.

"Good morning," Ellen said. "Or is it after-noon?"

I glanced at my watch. It was one o'clock. Since I'd had that enormous breakfast at the burger place, I wasn't hungry, but I was surprised that Roddy didn't seem to be. Unless, of course, he'd eaten.

"It's one o'clock," I said. "Roddy, have you had lunch?"

"Sure."

"We had a delicious stew cooked by Miranda," Ellen said. "I'm sorry you couldn't join us."

I met her piercing eyes and realized that, by speaking formally, as though this were a manor house, and she the lady of the manor, and a luncheon had been served in the dining room by a maid and a butler, she was reminding me of my manners. "I'm sorry, too," I said.

The gray head with the bun nodded. "Did you have lunch with your aunt, or with friends?"

In my mind I saw the burger shop and Ted.

"I had a late breakfast at the burger shop with Ted Lockwood," I said to Roddy. "Does that name mean anything to you?"

"Sure. He's the guy in the burger shop."

Then Ellen astounded me. "He's also a friend of ours."

"He is? I mean—how come? I thought you said you never saw anybody."

"We don't. You two and Ted are the only people

for a long, long time, except, of course, for a great friend, and for that terrible man who wanted to take our house away."

Roddy looked up. "Who was that?"

"An awful person. We thought at first he might be a friend, too, lending us money to pay the taxes—there was a special sewer assessment tax we couldn't meet. But then he threatened us. . . . I don't even want to think about it."

"What did he threaten you with?" Roddy asked. "You mean he had a gun and held you up?"

"Oh no, nothing as simple as that." She put down her brush and leaned back. "He simply said that his company would have to be repaid immediately for the money they'd lent us, instead of over a long period, as had been our understanding. And that the only way we could possibly pay them would be to sell this house and land—land that's been in our family for over one hundred years."

"Well, maybe you could have bought something smaller and easier to keep up," I said.

"Where?" The hawklike face poked at me. "In some terrible modern apartment house? Where we couldn't have had our animals? Where Miranda couldn't have her garden? If she'd been well, like other people . . ." And then the regal old woman seemed to remember she was talking to two children. "But I mustn't bother you with this. How silly of me. Young people should enjoy their lives and be free of worry."

"I like this place," Roddy said defiantly, and I realized he was talking to me. "I think Ellen and Miranda are absolutely right. Who'd want to live in one of those creepy modern places with everybody seeing everything you do and talking about it all the time."

A sudden practical thought occurred to me. "How do you get food here? That is, if nobody comes."

"There are people—sometimes young people— that the store gets to deliver things for us. Ted did that for a while. We never let any of them in, of course, except Ted. We watch for them, and Miranda meets them at the gate. But Ted was nice and liked our books and animals."

I took a deep breath. "He's also the son of the

man who did his best to destroy our father. I just found out today."

"What do you mean? What kind of a man?" Ellen said.

"A newspaperman," I said. "A Columnist."

"Well, what does that have to do with your father?"

"He's in jail, that's what it has to do!" I was angry about Ted's father, angry about Roddy's refusal to deal with his problem and angry that therefore I had to deal with it. "He made our father sound like some kind of horrible rich tyrant grinding the faces of the poor. And he did it again and again in his miserable paper."

Roddy went on stroking Sebastian. "Yeah, well, that doesn't mean that Ted's bad. Remember Tiger, and how he helps him."

"Tiger's asleep in the back room," Ellen said. "Ted brought him here this morning. He always brings him when Tiger starts showing up at the food place and getting Ted into trouble."

"I didn't know that. Why didn't you tell me?" Roddy said.

"You didn't ask. You just came in here and sat down and picked up the book."

Roddy got up. "I'm going back to see him."

As Roddy started towards the door, I said, "Just a minute. I have to talk to you."

"I'll go and see Tiger first."

"Roddy!"

The stubborn, closed-in look that I knew well settled over his face, and he walked out of the room.

"I'm sorry about your father," Ellen said. And then, in a gentle voice, "Do you want to talk about it?"

"No. Sometime I'd like to tell you about it, but not now."

I stared at the door, put a foot forward and then decided not to follow Roddy. Instead, I strolled around the room and started looking at the books. The ones I examined all seemed very old-fashioned, and I hadn't heard of any of them. Once I pulled a book off the shelf, and a cloud of dust seemed to fill the air. I sneezed.

"A little dust never hurt anyone," Ellen said, exactly as she had before. I turned around and looked at her. And then suddenly, at the same moment, we laughed.

"It's not entirely true, of course," she said. "Dust can be extremely harmful to anyone who has asthma. Luckily that's one thing that neither Miranda nor I has." There was an odd, dry note to her voice.

I heard myself say, "Why do you live like this?" And then was shocked by myself. I was fifteen, and Ellen was old . . . how old I didn't know, but more than old enough to be my grandmother. A lot of people—Aunt Marian, certainly—would think me rude, nosy and impertinent, the last a word used frequently by various nannies that Roddy and I had had. I also realized it was a question that I couldn't have asked Miranda, and that was the difference between the two women.

"Because . . . because I'm afraid of what might happen if we tried to change." She looked around her. "However . . . decrepit . . . this place seems to you, we're used to it. I told you, when you asked why we didn't sell the place, that Miranda wouldn't have anywhere to keep her animals. Suppose we did get a house, or an apartment in suburbia—people would think we were strange. They might try to interfere. And neighbors would complain about the smell. It doesn't matter too much about me. They'd probably stick me in a hospital and I'd die there, and nobody, except Miranda, would be any the poorer. But then, what would happen to her?"

"But . . . what'll happen to her, anyway? I mean . . . well, she is younger than you, of course."

"Miranda is fifty. Not young. I'm seventy-eight. You mean what will happen to her when I die?"

"Yes."

"We have a great friend, Miranda and I. I mentioned him to you before. He's the executor of my will. He'll see to it that she will be able to be somewhere where she can keep her animals, and he won't let greedy relatives put her in a hospital where they'll shoot her full of medicines, poke around her secrets and take away everything that means anything to her—all in the name of humaneness. She's been in a couple of those places and she's not going again—not while I live. Nor afterwards." Tears brightened the fierce eyes.

"But—maybe she would get well."

"What's well? Medicated within an inch of her life, watched over, never free and with nothing to love?"

As if on cue, the fat elderly dachshund wandered in, wheezing.

"All right, Bismarck. You can have your cookie." And Ellen thrust her hand into one of the many bags around her and held something out in her hand. Bismarck waddled over and, breathing heavily, sat back on his haunches, paws up, in the classic begging position. Ellen balanced the morsel on the end of Bismarck's nose.

"Snap!" Ellen said.

Bismarck tossed the morsel up in the air and caught it. Then he sat down and with obvious satisfaction started to scrunch on it.

"Good dog!" Ellen said.

Bismarck swallowed the remains of the morsel and looked pleadingly at her.

"No. You're fat enough. What's troubling Roddy?"

For a moment I didn't realize she was addressing

me. Then the meaning of her question hit me. "Why do you think anything's wrong?"

"I can feel it. He's hiding from something. He wouldn't be here if he weren't hiding from something."

"He's hiding from his illness," I said finally. Roddy trusted Ellen as I had trusted Ted, so therefore it wasn't a betrayal.

"What illness?"

"He has . . . epilepsy. He's had seizures and is supposed to be on medicine. Mother told him to bring a big supply when we came over here. But he didn't. He had a bad time at school. Now he's made himself believe that because he hasn't had a seizure for a year and a half, and because the doctor said he might get over it, it's gone. It doesn't make sense! You'd think he'd do anything to keep that medicine on hand. If he had a seizure on the beach, in front of people . . . But he's talked himself into this attitude. You saw him walk out of the room."

"If he passionately doesn't want a thing to be there, then for him it isn't there," Ellen said. "I have a great sympathy for that way of dealing with things, having been rather given to it myself." She picked up some wools and held them against her painted canvas. "But you don't accept that, do you?" She glanced up. "What's the alternative?"

"I tried to call his doctor in England, but he's on vacation. Mother's traipsing around Europe. The druggist won't send a supply without the doctor telling him to. So the only thing is to tell Aunt Marian. Ted—"even to mention his name was painful, but I forced myself to go on—"Ted says that no doctor worth anything would give Roddy a prescription without doing tests and things, and we can't do that without Aunt Marian's knowing. But if Aunt Marian knows, then sooner or later everybody'll know."

"And it's fear of people knowing as much as fear of a seizure that's behind his attitude?"

I hadn't thought of it as clearly as that. Yet the moment she said it, I knew it was true. "Yes."

"Which may be one reason why he has this thing for animals, and why he hides here."

"But not all animal lovers are people who have something they're ashamed of."

"No. But it's a powerful motive for those who do. Animals aren't critical. They don't care if you're thin or fat, black or white, poor or rich, a success or a failure, beautiful or ugly. If they love you, they love you. It's very comforting. Don't you think that somewhere behind her fantasies and dreams Miranda knows that?"

"Is she really . . . is she mentally ill?"

Ellen's sharp eyes looked up at me. "I don't know the answer to that any more than you know what you ought to do about Roddy. When she was hospitalized, they gave her shock treatments and all kinds of medicine. When she got home, for a long time she just sat and stared at the wall. When you talked to her, she made sense—in a miserable way—but it was like talking through a mesh. Slowly she started going back to where she was—the way you see her now. The family—cousins and so on—wanted to put her away again. She pleaded with me not to do it. I had to make a decision then, so I did. This was an old family summer cottage. We came to live here nearly thirty years ago. Perhaps it was the wrong decision. But it's too late to go back. You do your best, Betsy, but you can't control everything. And that's what you're trying to do: control things so they'll come out right. When I was young, Americans had great scorn for people in other parts of the world who say 'It's the will of God' and then resign themselves to unpleasant situations, instead of trying to get out of them. There's a lot to be said for the American attitude. But there's a little to be said for the other." She'd been tying the sheaves of wool strands together. Now she looked up at me. "So what are you going to do? Tell your Aunt Marian? That's what your dilemma is, isn't it? Let Roddy risk the consequences of his stubbornness, or tell your aunt and suffer those consequences."

It was neatly stated. Either or. "What would you do?" I asked.

"Oh no, Betsy. This is your dilemma. It must be your decision."

We didn't say anything for a while. Bismarck gave up hoping for another morsel and went to sleep, snoring loudly.

Finally I got up and went to the back of the house. Roddy was in the studio with Tiger and a large rabbit I hadn't seen before. It was sitting in the middle of the floor, and a trail of black pellets led to it from across the wooden floor. No wonder the place smelled, I thought. Tiger was lying on his back, four paws in the air, with Roddy scratching his stomach. With his other hand Roddy stroked the rabbit's long ears. I had been standing there, watching for a few minutes, when it occurred to me that Miranda was quietly singing as she painted. I listened to the words. What I heard was something that sounded like "Rum stum stiddle dum, dum taddle dumstead. . . ."

"What's that song?" I asked. It had a catchy tune.

Miranda took the paintbrush out of her mouth. "Just something I made up."

"It's nice. But I didn't quite catch the words."

"Never mind. Petal did."

"Petal?"

"Yes. On my lap. Also Charley."

I went over and looked. A small piece of fur zipped past me on the floor, ran up to the window and out.

I jumped. "What was that?"

"That was Charley. You frightened him."

"But what is he?"

"A squirrel."

"And who's Petal?"

"The thing on my lap that's making all the noise—apart from me, that is."

With that she stopped singing, and I saw what she was referring to. Petal was a kitten of about three months, with a purring mechanism that would not have disgraced a sports car.

"She likes to hear me sing," Miranda said in her dreamy voice, and resumed her song.

"Can you tell me what the words are?"

" 'Rum stum stiddle dum, dum taddle dum'. . . . Or is that the first verse?"

For a moment there was silence, then the kitten suddenly sat up and stretched.

"You see," Miranda said. "She likes to hear me sing. That's why she sleeps so peacefully. Now she's awake."

"I think that's silly," I said.

Miranda made a long sweep on her paper.

"You do?" Then she sang in rhythm:

"Well, it's your right
To think as you like.
Rum, tum, te tum *Ta!*"

"Roddy," I said, "let's go."

"No. I'm going to stay here until dinner."

"Do you want me to tell Aunt Marian that you've run out of medicine?"

Roddy looked at me. "If you do, I won't speak to you—forever."

"That's crazy. You could have a seizure—at any moment."

"I don't need it anymore."

"Then it's on your head," I said. "I won't tell Aunt Marian and I won't mention it again. If you have a seizure, it's your own responsibility. I'm not going to have anything more to do with it. Hear?"

Roddy didn't say anything. He just went on stroking the two animals.

"I said, do you hear?"

"I hear you."

I stood there for a while, but he didn't say anything more. Miranda went on with her funny little tune. From where I was standing I could see the garden, with its incredible colors, like a shaggy, unkempt, magnificent shawl.

"Okay. I'm going. If you know what's good for you, you better be back at the house for dinner." The place was beginning to get me down. There was a quality about the house and about Ellen and Miranda that was powerfully attractive—as though in it I would never again have to struggle. Everything was settled, and anyway, none of it mattered.

None of what? I wondered.

I went towards the door and was almost through it when Roddy said, "If Ma thought it was so important for me to have the medicine, why didn't she make sure I'd packed it?"

"Come on, Roddy, you know the answer to that."

"Yeah, well, I don't need the bloody stuff anymore."

"That's a dirty word," Miranda said.

Roddy grinned. "Bloody? Why should 'bloody' be dirty? People say they have bloody noses or bloody hands all the time."

"Because it doesn't mean 'bloody.' It's a corruption of an old oath, 'By our Lady.' You mustn't say that. It's wicked."

"Pooh!" Roddy said.

"If you say that, you mustn't come back here. The red knight wouldn't like it."

"Who's the red knight?"

"Look around you!" Miranda made a sweeping gesture and knocked over her paints.

"Thank you, dear," she said sweetly to Roddy, who was picking them up. I watched my young brother place the tubes and brushes back on top of the crate. I could see now why Miranda used it. Without its bottom and one side, the crate was the right size and shape to fit over her lap. Slapping everything on the top of the crate, Roddy sat down again next to Tiger and turned his attention to the rabbit. He didn't look at me. I tried to remember if he had ever picked up anything that I had spilled.

"Okay," I said. "It's your decision. And it's your risk."

I was about to leave when I remembered the red knight and looked up at the walls. There he was, going through adventure after adventure in the paintings tacked to the wall.

"Is there a story going through the paintings?" I asked.

Miranda stopped humming. "Of course. Can't you see it?"

"No."

"Then it's not for you. It's only for people who understand."

"Understand what?"

"You are being extremely hostile. If you don't leave, I shall have to take steps."

"What steps?" I thought she was being ridiculous, and I suppose my voice showed it.

"I shall turn you into a frog, a female frog. And let me tell you that's extremely serious. No amount of kissing can turn a female frog into a prince—or a princess."

"You're—"

Suddenly she turned around and looked at me.

Her dark eyes blazed. "Go!" she said. "You have bad vibrations today."

I waited to see if Roddy would stick up for me, but he didn't. So I left.

Chapter Seven

When I told Aunt Marian that Ted was picking me up at seven for dinner, her nostrils arched a little. "I really don't know what you see in him," she said. "But I assume he's all right. Please be back no later than eleven."

"All right."

Ted arrived promptly, wearing a dark sports shirt and chinos.

"Ted Lockwood," he said, offering his hand to Uncle Paul on the porch, before I could make the introductions. I was not going to mention his last name, but since he had, I waited to see if there was a reaction. There was.

"Any relation to Max Lockwood?" Uncle Paul asked.

"Yes. He's my father."

"Well," Uncle Paul said, getting up and waddling to the bar, "your dad sure did a job on Betsy's dad." He turned to me. "Or didn't you know that?"

"Yes. I knew."

"I am really shocked that you would go out with Ted," Aunt Marian said.

"Betsy probably has her reasons," Uncle Paul put in.

Ted's wide mouth was tightly closed.

"Good night, Mrs. MacTiernan," he said to Aunt Marian. He held open the screen door for me. "Good night, sir," he said to Uncle Paul.

The evening was off to a bad start. We walked along the beach. I had on white pants, a blue sports shirt and sandals, and the loose sand trickled over and under my toes. Ted had on sneakers.

"Would you rather walk on the road?" he asked after a bit.

"No. I don't mind sand. I like it."

We walked some more; then Ted said, "We can talk about it now, or wait until after we've eaten. Which would you rather?"

"Whatever you say." I felt miserably torn. I was sure, somehow, that the moment we really started in on the subject of his father and mine, that would be the end of the relationship. But I also didn't want it to end. When I thought about Ted's father, I was furious. When I looked at Ted himself, he was like somebody I'd half dreamed of, but whose face I'd never actually seen. To my own astonishment, I put out my hand and took his. We stopped. Ted turned to face me. We were on the wide, flat beach, visible for miles around. Yet we just stood there, our hands locked together.

"I don't want us to fight," Ted said. "I like you a lot. More than any girl I've ever known."

All I could say was, "Me too. I mean, I feel the same way about you."

I knew, then, that if he'd leaned forward to kiss

me, I would have kissed him back, and to heck with whoever might be watching. But he didn't.

"There's a fish place at the other end of the mall," he said. "Small and not very elegant, but they have the best fried fish I've ever eaten. Want to try it?"

"Love to."

It was as though we'd drawn a circle around the subject of our fathers, isolating it, putting it outside our lives for the moment. But both of us knew that it couldn't stay out there permanently.

At dinner we talked about everything else: about Ted's going to Columbia in New York City in the fall, about the fact that I had no idea where Roddy and I would be going. About Roddy's illness, and about Ellen and Miranda.

"They're funny old birds, crazy, but sort of nice," Ted said. "Well, I'll amend that. Ellen isn't really crazy. I guess I'd call her eccentric."

"But Miranda is?"

Ted's gray eyes were clear behind his glasses, the lashes black around them. "She's certainly had a couple of breakdowns in the past when she tried to cope with living what is generally called an ordinary life. What I think she's done here is invented a life that suits her better than any she could live today in an ordinary house, in an ordinary community and with ordinary friends. Whether that's crazy or not, technically speaking, I don't know. Maybe it's just canny. Try a little ketchup with that."

"This is terrific. You're right, the fish is marvelous." After a while I said, "Are they really recluses? I mean, I know they keep to themselves. But do other people know they're there? Does anybody ever *try* to see them?"

"Originally, so the story goes, a few of the older families tried to call. But as the Whitelaw house got dirtier and more run-down, and Ellen and Miranda collected more and more animals and got stranger and stranger, contact ceased. But not till after some kind of furor. One well-meaning, meddling woman decided that both should be institutionalized for their own good—in a private place, of course. But Ellen told her to get out of their house in no uncertain terms, and said that neither she nor Miranda was going anywhere to any institution. Miranda had been in one before, and Ellen was convinced that she came home worse, not better. It was after that that they simply withdrew. They deliberately let the outside of the house get the way it is. Ellen once said, 'It puts people off. Which is what we want.' "

"But from what they said, somebody once tried to take their house away, and somebody else came and rescued them."

"Yeah." Ted finished the last of his fish and started wiping off his hands, which, since the food was served in a basket and was meant to be eaten with fingers, took two napkins and one of those packaged moist towels.

"I've never figured out exactly what happened. Something to do with an assessment on their property. What with the new vacation houses and motels, the town decided to switch from the old cesspool to a regular sewage system and levied an assessment on all the property owners. Of course Ellen and Miranda didn't have the money, so they were sitting ducks for some loan shark who came along and lent it to them. Then, later, whoever it was demanded back the whole principal, plus heavy interest, immediately. If they didn't get it, they said they'd take the house and turn the women out, and showed all kinds of papers claiming their legal rights."

"Could they do that?"

"Who knows? Ellen didn't. She and Miranda panicked, then—presto—along came a rescuer who got them out of hock. I think, but I'm not sure, that that's the red knight that Miranda paints pictures of. She's made up a whole legend, but won't say what it is."

"I know. I asked her what the story of the red knight was, and she told me she'd turn me into a frog and that I had bad vibrations and should go! I felt like she thought she was exorcizing me, or something."

"Yes, she's very secretive about the red knight. My own view is that she developed a crush on him." Ted drank some coffee. "You know, the Whitelaws were a pretty prominent family in the last century and the early part of this. They had New Jersey Congressmen and judges and one governor. Ellen and Miranda are the last name holders. My dad heard about them, and was all set to do a column on them, on the general theme of 'How are the mighty fallen,' and/or '*Sic semper tyrannis.*'" He grinned. "It took me a while to talk him out of it. . . ."

Later, when everything between Ted and me had been destroyed, I thought about that moment there in the fish restaurant. We sat at a table in a corner, surrounded by windows that looked out on the ocean. The tables were plain, unstained wood; the food—or the remains of it—was in the baskets; there was sawdust on the floor. Outside, the lights from buoys blinked and through the open windows came the *shush-shush-shush* of the tide. It was really lovely, quiet and almost tender. And it was that moment that I took the wrong turn. I think Ted had forgotten the problem of our fathers when he spoke, but of course he had remembered by the time he finished his sentence. So the subject was back with us. Dinner was finished. There was nothing to stop us talking about it.

If . . . if I had just started to explain about my own father in the same tone and voice that Ted had used, when describing how he had dissuaded his father from doing a piece on the Whitelaws . . . If I had just not come on like an avenger . . . but I did.

All my anger at the newsmen and newswomen who had surrounded the apartment during the pretrial period . . . at the slanted editorials, at the distortions, and at Max Lockwood's regular pounding in his column . . . all of that rushed to the front.

"I guess he specializes in attacking people who can't defend themselves. I'm not sure I wouldn't rather have a father in jail than a father who did that."

Ted's eyes became as cold as stone. "I said we had to talk about it. Not fling unfounded accusations."

"It's not unfounded. Only nobody tried to find out the truth. That accountant lied. I know he lied. If your father is for the underdog, like that man at the motel said, why didn't he look into that?"

"I'd hardly call a rich business tycoon the underdog. Some underpaid accountant fits that description a lot better."

"How do you know he was underpaid? Father always paid his employees *well.* He knew what it was like to start from the bottom."

"And how do you know the accountant lied? Why should he?"

We were almost shouting at each other.

"Well, why didn't your father, the great investigator, bother to find out? Just because it sells more newspapers to attack somebody like my father?"

I heard my own voice as though it were that of a stranger. Why was I saying all this? Why was I being as insulting as I knew how to Ted—Ted whom I really liked, more than liked, even now?

He got up. "Dad sometimes gets carried away. But he's a careful—and honest—journalist. He checks his facts. He's one of the fairest people I know. And I'm not going to listen to this hysterical diatribe. I'll take you home."

I got up. "You don't have to. I can see myself home."

"Oh no! If you should turn your ankle on the way, given the way you and your relatives think, it'll be Dad's fault. I'm going to deliver you intact to your door."

"I'd rather go alone," I said, lying through my teeth.

"So go! I'll walk behind your ladyship. But I'll see you home."

By the time we were halfway there, I knew what an idiot I'd been. I wanted to turn around and put my head on his shoulder. I wanted to take his hand. I wanted . . . but I knew it wasn't any use. I'd seen his eyes, cold, and as distant as the horizon. I could imagine his scorn. . . . And there was my father, alone in a jail cell. I suddenly realized that when I thought of freedom, I thought of my father. He was—or had been—the freest person I'd ever known, unbound by so many things that seemed to shackle other people.

As I reached the porch steps, I looked back. Ted was standing straight and tall, watching me go in.

I finally said, "Good night. Thanks for seeing me home."

He didn't reply. He was still standing there when I went inside.

"Well," Aunt Marian said. "You're home early. How was it?"

I clenched my teeth. "Fine. He had work to do."

"As I said before you left—" she started.

But I couldn't bear it. "I have a terrible headache, Aunt Marian. I'm going to bed. Good night."

I lay in bed clenching my teeth together so hard my jaws ached. Consciously, I loosened them. "Are you a clencher or a grinder?" the orthodontist had politely inquired one time. Roddy and I had giggled about that for months. I realized now I was a clencher, along with all the other bad things I was, quick tempered and bossy (Roddy's favorite word for me). . . . Well, I argued, who else was going to take care of things?

But I couldn't help thinking of Ellen's words: "You do your best, Betsy, but you can't control everything. And that's what you're trying to do: control things, so they'll come out right. . . ."

The item appeared the next morning.

When I got downstairs, I found *The Beach Gazette*, folded, at my place. As I reached out to take it, Aunt Marian appeared in the doorway to the kitchen.

"Before you look at that, Betsy, I want you to know that there's a piece in it about you and Roddy being here, and also the fact that you're the children of Geoffrey Smith, currently in prison for tax fraud."

My hand was out, ready to pick up the paper. A horrible thought struck me. What was it that motel man had said? That Ted was a stringer for a local paper.

"Is there a by-line?" I asked.

"No. It's just a regular story. I thought you should know about it and brace yourself accordingly."

I snatched up the paper. The story was on the front page and simply reported the fact that we were here, staying with Mr. and Mrs. Paul MacTiernan, and that our father was at the moment in prison for tax fraud. I read it twice, then put the paper down. Across the table from me, Roddy was pushing cereal around his bowl.

"Did you read it?" I asked him.

"Yeah."

"Did it upset you?"

His green eyes looked across at mine. "Why? People were bound to find out anyway. Why are you so bothered? Are you ashamed?"

"No, of course not." I could feel both him and Aunt Marian looking at me.

"You look bothered," Aunt Marian said.

I was. Terribly. But I was feeling sick because I was terribly afraid that Ted had placed that news item. Which meant that I'd been wrong about him from the beginning.

Roddy started to slide away from the table. "See you later," he said, and turned towards the porch door.

"Roddy, where are you going this early?" Aunt Marion asked.

His eyes flickered towards me. "To play with some kids on the beach. I met them yesterday."

I listened to the astonishing lie and saw Roddy fasten his gaze on me. As clearly as anything on earth, I saw he was trying to compel me to back up his lie.

Aunt Marian turned to me. "Do you know these people—these children, Betsy?"

Why didn't she just leave it at "people"? Then the lie I was about to tell wouldn't be so total. I could easily claim that I knew the "people," that is, Ellen and Miranda, that he was with. But no stretch of truth would make them "children."

"Yes," I said. "They're okay."

"Who are they anyway?"

"Just some kids I met, Aunt Marian," Roddy answered. "Their parents are staying in the cove—at the motel."

Roddy's honest look would not have shamed a seraph. Only I could read the telltale freckles, getting darker by the minute, as his face became whiter. Tell the truth and shame the devil, one of our nannies used to say. But suppose I said, "Roddy likes to be with those crazy Whitelaw women in their rundown house amid all their animals" . . . ? Aunt Marian would put her foot down in a second. Furthermore, she'd probably dig up some snooty kids somewhere that Roddy could play with, either on the beach or at her club, and if he got upset and still didn't have his medicine, he might have a seizure and be exposed, in front of everyone.

Both he and Aunt Marian were watching me. "That's right," I said. "They're a couple of families staying at the motel for a week or so, and both have children Roddy's age."

"As long as you're keeping an eye on him," Aunt Marian said. She went back into the kitchen.

"Thanks," Roddy whispered, and slipped through the porch door out onto the sand.

Aunt Marian came back into the dining room, carrying some polished silver with her. "Who do you think wrote that news story?" she said. "I mean, who gave the paper the tip? Neither your uncle nor I have talked about the matter to anyone."

"I don't know."

"Well, personally, I suspect your friend Ted."

She was putting away the silver, but she raised her head and looked at me. "After all, his father is a newspaperman. It's in the family tradition, so to speak."

She closed the cabinet door. "I'm going over to the Club for bridge and lunch. You're welcome to come if you want. In view of that item, you might not want to."

If she hadn't made the last statement, I probably would have accepted. Something totally different would be a relief. But after those final words, I couldn't.

"No thanks. I think I'll just get a suntan on the beach," I said.

"Suit yourself."

I watched her go out the front door onto the concrete space by the garage door. Walter came out from the kitchen and held the door for her. Then they left.

I read the item again. No matter what I wanted to think, there couldn't be any doubt who had sent in that story. Strangely, although the previous night, when it was I who had behaved badly I had felt nothing but rage. Now, when I knew how wrong I had been about Ted and what a rotten fink he was, just like all newspaper people, I felt heartsick.

Finally I went upstairs, got some nail scissors, came down, clipped out the item and then sent it with a note to Ted via the burger shop. The note said, "Like father, like son. Congratulations on your first scoop!" I signed it "Betsy." Then I walked to the nearest mailbox and slipped it in.

What I wanted to do was to follow Roddy to the Whitelaw house. But Roddy's question, "Are you ashamed?" prevented me. Why? I argued to myself.

He was hiding, why shouldn't I? The answer came back like a tennis ball: because Roddy and I were—would be—hiding from different things. Roddy hid because of his illness. I would be hiding because of . . . because of Father. When I saw that, I knew the only thing I could do would be to go out onto the beach and stay there for the day. If people wanted to say something, or avoid me, let them.

I put on my new bikini, grabbed a couple of books, some oil and a pair of dark glasses, stuck them in a beach bag, along with a towel, and went downstairs.

The beach was crowded, more so than I'd seen it before. And I saw right away that Larry Babcock was up in the big lifeguard's chair.

Well, I thought defiantly, that's fine. I chose a central spot where everybody could see me, put the towel down, sat and took out one of the books. "Hurray for me," I said quietly to myself. It was a little pep cheer that I gave myself when I was feeling particularly unsure. "And hurray for Father, and for Roddy." Then I made up a new verse:

"In thunder, lightning and in rain,
We three folk supreme shall reign. . . ."

And then I wished Ted were there to appreciate it. I could imagine so easily the way his eyes would crinkle up at the corners. . . . But it wasn't any use thinking that. As far as I was concerned, he was the newest member of the Benedict Arnold society. . . . Creep, I thought to myself, and then decided not to think about it again, for the rest of the day, week, year. As I made this resolution, I found myself gazing far to my right, where the hamburger shop, squat and red, stood at the edge of the mall.

"Read!" I instructed myself, and saw I'd been holding the book upside down. Quickly, hoping nobody had noticed, I turned it right side up.

An hour later not one soul had come up to talk to me. I didn't know what to make of that: whether they had decided I was a true outcast, or were simply being too polite to question me.

But around noon another muscled young man came up to the lifeguard platform, and Larry jumped down. Evidently the watch was changing. I noticed all this out of the corner of my eye. Larry walked away, out of my line of vision. That's that, I thought, and reminded myself how much I disliked him.

"That was quite an item about you this morning in the local rag."

I swung around. Larry was standing in back of me, his torso smooth and tight with heavy muscles, and deeply tanned.

"Yes," I said.

"Too bad about your old man being in the slammer. That's got to be a first for the beach. We've had the cousin of the Secretary of State, and the daughters of two governors, but never anything as chic as the daughter of a jailbird."

I looked at him as steadily as staring up at the sun would let me. "My father is innocent, and I'm very proud of him. And you've got to be the world's greatest creep to say that to me. Or maybe you couldn't bear the idea that I didn't want to go out with you." Deliberately I pitched my voice loud enough for people around to hear. They were all pretending to read or gaze into the ocean's depths. I knew better.

There was a pause, then, "All right. Sorry I insulted your old man. Is that better?"

I ignored him.

"Leave her alone, Larry. Don't you know she prefers the hired help?"

I kept my eyes on my book, but was pretty sure I recognized the voice of the girl who had been in the burger shop talking to Larry when I first met him. She was a knockout brunette, and something told me she didn't like competition.

"That's pretty funny," Larry said. "Considering the hired help is our local newshawk."

I gritted my teeth and decided to sit it out.

Another pause, then, "Well, well, well," Larry said. "The media have arrived. Betsy, you're famous. Get up and pose for the cameras."

It never occurred to me he was being anything but nasty. And then I heard a man's voice. "Hey, is that the Smith kid sitting there? Come on, Irv. Let's get a shot from here. That's quite some body she has."

I spun around and then somehow leaped to my

feet. Everything seemed to happen at once. A man was advancing on me with a mike in his hand. Another man, balancing a camera on his shoulder, was following. Somebody yelled, "Get that dog out of the way."

I looked down. A dog I recognized immediately as Tiger was having the time of his life with a ball. Larry aimed a foot at him.

"Off, pooch! Let's not spoil the picture." It was some kind of weird remake of a scene that had been acted before, in the burger shop.

And then I saw Roddy. Looking sturdy and determined in his jeans and blue T-shirt, he was advancing on Tiger.

"There's the other Smith kid," somebody said. "We can get 'em together."

"Come on, Tiger," Roddy said, his voice agitated. "Let's go."

"Hold it, kid!" The man with the camera said. I knew the camera was on me, too, but I was watching Roddy.

"Roddy, it's all right. Let them get their stupid pictures." Somehow, without knowing how I knew,

I felt something terrible was about to happen. "Roddy, it doesn't matter. It's okay. Let's go in and have some lunch."

But it was too late. I saw Larry pick up the ball and with his powerful arm throw it towards the sea, where the breakers were crashing against the sand. The ball went into the wave behind the cresting front. Tiger took off running, his tail flat out. Roddy hurled himself after him, calling, "Hey, Tiger. Watch out!" I ran after them. Those were big waves for a slight dog. But that wasn't what was bothering me. I was remembering how the doctor had told me to watch Roddy carefully when he was in the water. If he had a seizure there, he could drown.

I heard Larry laughing behind me, as he was running to catch up with us. Tiger plunged into the first breaker and disappeared.

"Roddy!" I screamed, still running. But Roddy had disappeared, too.

It seemed like miles and hours before I reached the water. I heard the new lifeguard's whistle. But

I paid no attention. Then I saw Tiger's head, above the water. Thank God, I thought. But I couldn't find Roddy's. Then I saw him, his red hair coming up for a moment from the water, his arm around Tiger's neck.

Then the arm was flung up. I heard Roddy give a strange cry. I was in the water now, swimming frantically. Almost immediately I found Roddy and felt the convulsive thrusts of his legs. But I was older and a lot taller. Managing to get an arm around him, I thrust his chin above the water. Luckily, I was only a foot or two from being able to stand on the sand, and as soon as my feet touched bottom, I raised Roddy as high as I could and staggered out.

Then the next thing I knew, I was bending over him as he thrashed on the sand.

"Let me get to him," the lifeguard said. "I know what to do."

"Get away," I said.

But the seizure was finally over, and Roddy was lying still, a dazed look in his eyes. Tiger ran up, shook himself so that he sprayed everyone in reach, then started licking Roddy's face.

I knelt there, looking down into Roddy's face, aware of the camera a few feet away. But I no longer cared. "Come along, Roddy," I said. "Everything's fine. Let's go home."

Chapter Eight

Roddy got up slowly, saw everything—the men, the cameras, the people standing around. I took his hand.

"Let's go home," I said again. And we started to walk. People were standing in a sort of half circle several yards away from us. It felt like miles to get past them. Roddy's face was white, his freckles almost chocolate-colored.

"Look, miss," one of the men said. "I'm sorry, but I have to ask you . . ."

I gripped Roddy's hand and we got past them. "Miss . . ."

"For goodness' sake. Can't you leave them alone? What are you, sadists?" It was a woman's voice, but I didn't know whose.

"Look," the man said. "It's my job—"

"Scummy job," somebody else said. The voices were getting fainter, but we heard that much.

Suddenly Larry was walking beside us. "Look," he said. "I'm sorry. I didn't know—"

"Just get away," I said. "Please, *please*, leave us alone."

Larry stopped and turned back. Curiously, off to one side, I saw some kids Roddy's age for the first time. Two girls and a boy were standing there, one of them holding a beach ball. I saw Roddy look up and then down again, as we plowed through the sand to the cottage.

Where's Tiger? I wondered, and at that moment, as though he'd heard my question, Tiger rushed past and flung himself on Roddy. Roddy put his hand down and ruffled his ears. Tiger jumped up, and Roddy put his arms around him and hugged him.

"Can we take him home for now?" Roddy said.

"Yes."

"Aunt Potty—"

"If Aunt Potty opens her mouth I'll . . . I'll shove an ashtray down it." And the funny part was, I felt strong enough and angry enough to do just that.

"I hope Ted doesn't go looking for Tiger at Ellen's," Roddy said. "Maybe we ought to call him and say we have him."

"You can if you want." I felt like telling Roddy what a rat fink Ted turned out to be . . . how he was responsible for the news item in the paper, which brought the camera team. But Roddy didn't need to hear it right now.

"Maybe later." Roddy sounded tired.

"Why don't you rest," I said.

"Okay."

When we got back to the beach house, Roddy went straight upstairs, with Tiger following him.

Cinda, who had come into the hallway when we came in, said, "You know Mrs. MacTiernan doesn't allow dogs in the house, Miss Betsy."

"She will this time," I said. "Go on up, Roddy. It's okay."

I wanted to make sure he got out of his wet clothes, and I wanted to change mine. When I was dry, I came down again. Then I went into the kitchen and told Walter and Cinda what had happened.

"Oh, that poor little boy," Cinda said. "He must feel awful."

"He does. And right now he's very tired. When Aunt Marian comes home, I'll tell her Roddy has Tiger. If she wants to make a fuss, she can make a fuss."

At that moment the doorbell rang.

I heard Walter say, "I'll see if she wants to see you, but I don't think she ought to be bothered right now."

"That's that newsman," I said.

Walter came back into the kitchen. "Some man from a TV news station, Miss Betsy."

"He wants a statement? I'll give him a statement." I marched out to the front door.

"All right. Here I am. You saw what happened.

I suppose you're going to run that in every living room in the area tonight!"

"No, we're not. We're not monsters, Miss Smith, despite what you think. And anyway, one of the kids of our chief news editor has the same problem. It's no disgrace."

We stood there, facing one another. I was on the top step looking down. The cameraman was standing behind the reporter, the camera on his shoulder, but he wasn't filming anything. Up on the road was the van, with *WJNK News* on the side.

"What do you want?" I finally said.

"Well, we read the item in *The Beach Gazette* this morning and wondered if you would give us a statement. I'm sorry if it seems heartless, but there it is. That's what I've been sent out to ask."

"All right," I said. "I will."

The man with the camera got into position and the other man held a microphone in front of me. "I'm talking here to Betsy Smith, the daughter of the business tycoon who has just been jailed for tax fraud. Miss Smith, how do you feel—"

That was as far as he got. I took the mike out of his hands.

"My father is innocent," I said loudly into it. "Yes, technically it was his responsibility. But he didn't know about the fraud. That accountant lied. Why he lied I don't know. But I wish all the news media would help me find out, instead of hounding me and my brother. And my father. We're very proud of him." I finished on a loud note. Then I handed the mike back to the newsman and went in and slammed the door behind me.

"That's wonderful, Miss Betsy," Walter said.

"And we're proud of you." Cinda joined in.

"Thank you," I said, and burst into tears.

Roddy and Tiger came down around three.

"Hungry?" Cinda asked him. "I can make you a nice tuna fish sandwich."

"I guess I'm not too hungry," Roddy said. He was wearing his closed-in expression. "Thanks anyway." And he pushed open the back door. Tiger shot out. I followed.

"Roddy, are you going to see Ellen and Miranda?"

"Yes."

"It's a long walk."

"I can make it."

"I'll come with you." I knew Roddy didn't want me. I knew he wanted to be alone with Ellen and Miranda, and suddenly I understood why as I never had before. With Ellen and Miranda his illness didn't matter. They accepted him as he was. "I won't bug you about anything," I said. "At least, not now."

"Okay."

The walk was long. I could see how tired Roddy was. When we got there, after greeting everyone, animal and human, he lay down on the floor of Ellen's room and, with Tiger as his pillow, went to sleep. I sat on the sofa and started reading *The Jungle Books* and tried not to think about Ted.

After about half an hour, Ellen looked up from her drawing board. "He doesn't look himself," she said quietly.

"No. He isn't. He had a seizure today."

"What happened?"

"Everything. All at once. A television newsman and cameraman turned up. They saw the news item about our being here, and came to interview us."

"Why? Why would they want to interview you? Are you famous in some way I didn't know?"

"I told you. Our father is in jail. Son and daughter of famous business tycoon, jailed for fraud, staying here with uncle and aunt. That kind of thing."

Ellen didn't say anything for a moment, then she said, "That's despicable."

"I couldn't agree more. But it sells newspapers. You should have seen the reporters around our apartment after the indictment. They were like vultures."

I told her about Roddy and how he lay on the beach afterwards, thrashing, and how everybody stood around watching.

Ellen said, "You're a good girl, Betsy." After a pause she added, "Was your aunt there?"

"No. She was at her club. But she'll have heard

by now." I didn't say anything for a minute. "At least she'll make Roddy go to a doctor."

"What did you say?" Roddy said, coming to suddenly.

"Just that you're going to have to go to a doctor, Roddy. You know you will."

He sat up, and stared into space for a moment. "Maybe I'll just stay here. Maybe I won't go back."

"Roddy," Ellen said, "you have to go to a doctor and get medicine again. After that, you'll be fine. You're welcome to be here. But you can't hide here. Do you understand? It doesn't do any good."

"You're hiding," Roddy said, with more perception than I'd given him credit for. "Aren't you?"

"Yes. But you have a choice, Roddy. People with your illness can live full, useful lives. I didn't think Miranda and I had one. There's a big difference." There was a silence. Tiger sat up and started scratching. "You know, Roddy, if you just accept it and go on, it won't be as bad as you think it is."

There was a much longer pause. Then Roddy

said, "Yeah, okay. Come on, Tiger. Let's go see Miranda."

Seeing Tiger's plumy black tail disappear through the doorway made me think of Ted. My heart gave a funny unhappy jerk.

"What time does Ted come to pick up Tiger?" I asked.

"Anytime after three, usually. Why?"

"Because I don't want to be here when he comes. He's responsible for what happened this morning."

"What on earth are you talking about?"

"I'm talking about our local newshawk, Ted Lockwood. He's the one who put that item in the paper. He acts as a stringer for them."

"You must be mistaken. He wouldn't do that."

"Wouldn't he? Why not? That's the kind of thing his father did to my father. 'Business tycoon Geoffrey Smith jailed for tax fraud. Robs employees.' It's a rotten lie. But that didn't stop him from writing it."

The silence went on for so long that I turned and looked at Ellen. There was a strange expression on her face. Then she said, "You said Geoffrey Smith?"

"Yes. That's Father's name. Why?"

"You're Geoffrey Smith's children?"

"Yes. Why, Ellen? What's the matter?"

"Geoffrey Smith is the man who rescued us. Betsy, my dear . . ." Her mouth twisted. "He's Miranda's red knight."

Chapter Nine

We stared at each other. What Ellen said made no sense. "What do you mean?"

"The red knight—in the paintings on the studio wall."

"You mean the knight with the red hat?"

"Yes, only it's not a hat. It's his hair. As you know, Miranda doesn't draw very well."

I stood there for what seemed a long time. The house was absolutely quiet. Finally I became aware that Ellen was leaning forward, asking me a question. "Why is your father in jail? Did you say something about tax fraud? If you did, it's utter nonsense. Geoffrey Smith would never do anything like that."

"I wish you owned a newspaper and would print that as a headline every day," I said bitterly. "But what do you mean, 'rescued' you?" It still didn't sound real.

Ellen sat back. "That was long ago," she said. "Geoffrey used to work around here when he was young. Did you know that?"

"I know that it was here that he met Mother. She and Aunt Marian used to vacation here—not in the house my aunt and uncle are in now, but another."

"Yes. He started his first plant here. He set it up in an abandoned building. I don't understand business, and I don't know what went wrong. But something did, and he ran out of money. We—Miranda and I—knew him, because before he had this business, he used to work in a garage, and we had a car then. Somehow we became friends. He used to do odd jobs for us. There wasn't anything he couldn't fix. When he was here, this house was always in repair and freshly painted—at least on the inside. We couldn't pay him much, but he liked doing it.

"Anyway, he ran into trouble and came here to tell us about it. This was long before he was married, and I don't think he had too many confidants. If he couldn't get twenty thousand dollars in a hurry, he'd have to close the plant. Well . . . we weren't as poor then, and there were still things we could sell. We didn't tell him what we intended to do . . . but we were grateful to him for being our friend at a time when everybody wanted to tell us how to run our lives. Anyway, we sold a valuable carpet and two paintings. And the next time he came, we gave him the money.

"He didn't want to take it at first, but he did, and swore he'd pay it back with interest—which he did, within two years. That must be nearly . . . nearly thirty years ago. He met your mother and married her and invited us to the wedding. But by that time we had . . . retired. He even offered to bring your mother here, but I think he knew we didn't want that. Only certain kinds of people are right for this house, and he and I both knew she probably wasn't one of them." Ellen's old eyes focused on me. "I mean no offense, my dear. But—"

"Yes. It's all right. I understand. You were right, she isn't . . . wasn't . . ." And then I felt disloyal. "It doesn't have anything to do with . . . Well, I mean, I love her very much, but—"

"Yes," Ellen interrupted. We both understood.

"What happened then?"

"Nothing, for a long time. We extracted from him the same kind of promise we have from you and Roddy—that he'd keep the house and everything about it secret. He'd send us Christmas cards and occasional packages. He always said he'd make the trip back to see us, but he started taking over other businesses and never managed to return.

"Then, suddenly, or it seemed as if it was suddenly, our money ran out. Miranda and I have never been very good at seeing ahead. And of course we couldn't foresee that the town would levy an assessment on the property when they decided to build a new sewage system. Anyway, we didn't have enough to pay the assessment and pay our usual expenses, small as they are. I managed to get myself into town, somehow—actually by local taxi—and went to the bank we'd always dealt with. But they couldn't give us a loan. We were in despair when a man, very pleasant and smooth-talking, came here, said he'd heard we were in trouble and offered to lend us the money."

Ellen's voice had become hoarse, and she cleared her throat. "Turn on the light, dear. I don't seem to see as well as I used to."

I turned on the light above her chair. "Go on, Ellen. That was the villain, wasn't it? The one who tried to take your house."

"Yes. Afterwards, of course, I knew we'd been fools. We should have looked into what he said more carefully. But he was very nice to Miranda and made her happy by praising some of her paintings. That should have alerted me, right there. But we were desperate, and I signed the papers he produced. Then he gave us the check.

"A year after that he suddenly turned up and told us we were way behind in our interest payments. We'd been paying him a monthly amount we'd agreed on, which was the principal. He'd never said a word about interest, and we hadn't asked. . . . He said that now, according to the papers we had signed, we owed a huge extra amount because the unpaid interest had compounded. However, he said, he had found somebody who would buy the property for almost as much as we owed him. We refused, of course.

"Then he said that if we wouldn't sell to his . . . friend, he'd sue us for failure to pay what we owed him, and take over the house. . . .

"Betsy, I still don't know what he'd have done. He said it was all in the contract I'd put my signature on, and when I asked to see it, brought it out of his pocket. I told him I had no memory of signing any such thing, but of course I knew and he knew that I had, and hadn't even bothered to read it. Betsy— never, never, never sign anything without reading it all through carefully."

"That's what Father's always told us."

"Well, he should know, especially now.

"I asked him to give us a week. He agreed to give us three days. Betsy, I didn't know whether by law he could take the house or not. But we didn't have the money to hire a lawyer to find out. And I was afraid of him. I knew then that he was probably a criminal. We don't read papers or listen to the radio or watch television. But even Miranda and I knew that there were gangsters who seemed respectable who did that sort of thing."

"Gangsters," I said. It seemed so old-fashioned, like a thirties movie on the late late show.

"Yes. What do you call them now?"

"The mob."

"I'd forgotten the word. That's what your father said. Well, I got together a little money and called the local taxi again and met him at the turn-off place in the woods. Then I went to a public phone in a hotel and called your father. He had told us where to reach him. We'd tried before, but he always seemed to be somewhere else—halfway across the world. And, of course, since we didn't have a phone, we couldn't leave a message for him to call back. Luckily, this time he was in the country. I didn't get him right away, of course, but I stayed at the phone booth until he called me back—which he did in about half an hour.

"He turned up that night, got all the details from us, and went and paid the full amount of the loan. He took a lawyer with him and demanded some kind of receipt. When he came back, he gave us a copy of the receipt and told us never to let anybody else bail us out.

"He wanted to fix up the house. But we didn't want that. So—he said to let him know when he could help us again and left.

"And now you must tell me. Why is your father in jail? What can we possibly do to help him?"

"Because of a rotten accountant who lied about him. I know he did." And I told Ellen what had happened to Father.

She sat there for a long time, gripping the arms of her big chair.

"*Cui bono?*" she said finally.

"What?"

"To whom the good? My father, who was something of a Latin scholar, used to say that. In other words, who benefited by incriminating your father?"

I sighed. "Father said, when we last saw him, that

the accountant was probably just trying to save his own skin. That he lied because he stole the money himself."

"I suppose it's possible," Ellen said grudgingly. "But from what you say, there seems to have been a tremendous furor. Tell me about the newspapers again."

"They made him look like a monster," I said bitterly, "especially Ted's father."

"Ted's a good boy," Ellen said. "He wouldn't have put that item in the paper about you and Roddy. After all, if he was just interested in a good story he could sell, he'd have told about Miranda and me long ago. Last members of a distinguished family living like derelicts. Oh yes, I haven't been out of the world that long. He could have made quite a sensation with a story like that. But he didn't."

Suddenly I remembered what he'd said about talking his father out of doing a story on the old ladies. "As a matter of fact," I said, "he talked his father out of doing a column on you. He told me that, just before we had our fight."

"You see? And if his father let himself be talked out of it, then he couldn't be such a monster, either. Perhaps it's just partiality for your father, but I'm sure there's something else there. We'll ask Ted when he comes."

I jumped up. "He—I'm sure he doesn't want to see me."

"When your father's good is concerned, you're going to let a little thing like that stop you?"

"No, of course not! It's just . . ." I saw Ellen's eyes, probing me.

"It's just what?"

"It's just that we . . . well, we seemed to like each other."

"Oh—well, we can't stop for that nonsense now. This is important."

I opened my mouth to tell her that it wasn't nonsense. But then I saw she was right. I would wait for Ted. After I made that decision, I saw how anxious it made me. But I also saw how glad I was.

Once I knew who the red knight was, I could figure out the legend that Miranda had woven around him, and her paintings, crude as they were, made sense. Actually, if you overlooked who the figures were supposed to be, there was a sort of mythic quality about the story . . . like the fairy tale of the princess who lay sleeping in a castle behind a wall of thorns, waiting for the right prince to come and wake her with a kiss. . . . And for the first time I noticed, in the corner of the first panels, before the red knight appeared, a frog, wearing a red hat. . . . Did she have the two fairy tales connected? The princess who had to kiss the frog before he could become a prince, and the princess who slept to be awakened by the prince . . . the same prince . . . ?

I thought about asking Miranda that. But then it would entail telling her that I now knew my father was the red knight. I got as far as saying, "Miranda."

But she said, "Hush, later. I am in the midst of creation. . . . And I'm still not sure about your vibrations."

"Why can't a female frog become a princess?"

"Because that's not in the story, of course."

She said it with so much scorn that I decided not to press the matter.

Ted arrived a little after four. I heard the back door open and close, and then his voice: "Tiger?"

There was the scrabble of paws, and then a body hurled itself through the studio to the front of the house, attended by much happy barking.

"Hello, Tiger," Ted's voice said. "Good boy! I brought you some hamburger."

Slowly I walked through the rooms to the front hall. "Hi!" I said.

Ted, who'd been on one knee, stood up slowly. I saw then, on the floor, the envelope, clipping and note I'd sent him.

"I can't believe the mail delivery is that good," I said. "I only mailed that this morning."

"No. I was talking to Willy, the mailman, when he opened the mailbox. So I grabbed it, and he said if I didn't tell anybody I could have it. Thanks a lot! You really do have a high opinion of me, don't you—along with everyone else! All the people in the hamburger joint seemed to think that it was my brilliant reporting that brought the TV newsmen this morning. And in view of what happened to

Roddy, that's made me as popular as a skunk at a party. Just to make you feel better, when the manager of the store heard about it, he fired me. Didn't ask if I was responsible for the item, just fired me."

"That's pretty scummy," I said. "I mean, without asking you first." But then, I thought, I hadn't either. "But I didn't either, did I?"

"No, you didn't."

"Did you place that item?"

"Do you care?"

"*Of course* I care."

There was a long silence.

"I care a lot," I said. "You ought to know that."

"No," he said, "I didn't."

We looked at each other. After a minute he stepped over Tiger. He took my hands, or maybe I took his. Then he kissed me. His lips were gentle. He smelled wonderful, and his cheek was a little bristly. I put my arms around him. He pulled me close.

"Let's start from scratch," he said. And there was that funny, husky note in his voice again. "But maybe we ought to have that talk about our fathers."

Everything came rushing back. "Oh, Ted, there's so much to tell you. Come into Ellen's room. My father's the red knight. And Ellen thinks, too, there has to be some reason why that accountant lied."

"What's this?" Ted said, as we walked into the front room.

Ellen and I, together and then separately, told Ted the whole story she'd told me. Finally we ran out of breath.

"It's funny," Ted said finally. "I called my father last night and told him about us and what you'd said about the accountant. I asked him if he'd bothered to check the guy out, and he said he hadn't—it looked like such an obvious abuse of big-business muscle to him. So I asked him if he would now—by this time he has contacts everywhere. Today when I spoke to him he said that the first few people he talked to made Lavall sound so holy, so much the fine, upstanding, moral citizen, that he could be considered ready for sainthood. So Dad dug deeper, this time among some minor hoods. And there was one guy who was ready to swear that Lavall was well known in Las Vegas among the gaming tables and owed money—a lot of money. That's all Dad had time to find out. But he asked me to ask you, Betsy, if your father had ever done anything to make anybody mad."

"Like who?"

"I don't know. But he was a businessman. Had he underbid anybody? Gotten a contract that somebody else was after? Maybe somebody whose business your father took over?"

"Why? I mean, what would that have to do with it?"

"Because if somebody had a grudge against your father, can you think of a better way to pay him back than to place somebody in one of his businesses to do just what that accountant did? I mean, he sure fixed him. I'll admit I wouldn't have thought of this, but Dad's been around. The moment he seriously considered your father might have been shafted, he hit on this. Particularly, he said, if whoever thought up this brilliant scheme had a local judge in his pocket, and especially if it was made to look like your father not only defrauded the government—which is bad, but lots of people do it—but betrayed his employees, too. That would turn public opinion against him. Do you see what I'm getting at?"

"I do," Ellen said. "My father used to write about that kind of thing. Betsy, go over to that big bureau and open the next-to-the-bottom drawer. I was going to throw away all the papers and bills connected with that awful man, but your father made me promise that I wouldn't. Somewhere, on something, is the name Lavall. But I can't remember on what. Anyway, it's in one of those drawers. I think it's the third, but maybe it's one of the others."

By this time Ted had jerked open the drawer and papers were streaming out. There was a scamper of feet and a mouse tore across the floor and into a mousehole, pursued by Bagheera, who crouched beside the hole.

Ted picked up a sheet of paper, looked at it carefully, then crumpled it up and stuffed it into the opening of the hole. "Just a piece of scrap paper," he told Ellen.

We finally went through the whole bureau. It was like going through a hundred giant wastebaskets.

The drawer was deep and stuffed with bills and receipts going back to before World War II.

We had taken the drawer over to Ellen's chair, partly because it was easier to do that than for her to move, and partly because the light near the desk wouldn't work. When Ted turned it on, it fell apart. The air was thick with dust. We all sneezed.

"A little dust never hurt anyone," I couldn't help saying. Ellen sighed.

At one point Roddy came in. "What are you up to?" he asked.

Ted and I tried to condense what we were doing and why. "Okay," Roddy said, "I'll help." He took a pile and started looking through it.

"Look at all the small print," Ellen said. "I know the name Lavall is on something."

"If we find it, what'll it prove?" Roddy said, turning what looked like an ancient invoice every which way and then over on the other side.

"It might—just might—prove there's a connection between what happened to your dad and his helping Ellen and Miranda out."

"But why?" I asked. "I'm happy to look, but I just don't see it."

"How much did you owe this shark, Ellen?" Ted asked.

"About twelve thousand dollars. The original assessment we couldn't pay was a little over six thousand. He said the rest was interest."

"All right," Ted said. "If we find what I think we might find, then some construction company would have bought one of the best pieces of land on this rich vacation coast for six thousand dollars. In an area of this size, they probably make it their business to find out who's in hock to the local government. And when the land is valuable, they could cook up a scheme like the one they tried on Ellen and Miranda. Once they've got the land, they could tear down the house, clear the woods down to the water, and build a resort or club, or vacation houses, and clean up millions. Your father did them out of that, Betsy—at least I think he did. And they paid him back. . . ."

The whole thing made horrible sense.

It was an hour later that Roddy found the paper we were looking for. "Is this it?" he said, and handed it to Ellen.

Ellen looked at it. "Yes, that's it. That's the receipt he gave me when I handed him the check for our taxes. The funny thing was, it was Miranda, who was having a bad spell then, who came out of what seemed almost like a trance and said, 'Get a receipt, Mummy.' Afterwards, when he'd gone, she said he was an evil man. I thought at the time that she was . . . well, having one of her mental flights. But I asked him to give us a receipt. It surprised him, but he took this piece of paper out of his pocket. You can see the letterhead. Armand Lavall Martin. Building and Construction Company. It was just a scrap of paper he had in his pocket. His name was Herbert Martin."

"I'll telephone this to Dad as soon as I get to a phone," Ted said.

"Do you really think it would help Father?"

Ted looked at me. "Possibly. Maybe even probably. If some connection can be established between the accountant who shafted your father and the people he paid off for Ellen, then maybe public pressure can force another investigation. It's worth a try, anyway." He gave a wry smile. "You ought to be the first to believe in the power of the press. Right?"

I couldn't help it. I laughed. "Right."

"I have to tell you, it may cost money. Private investigating—especially if you're in a hurry—usually does. Maybe your Uncle Paul—"

"I knew there was going to be some use for that five thousand!"

"What five thousand?"

"I'll tell you all about it later. But it's there. This is terrific, Ted!" I hugged him. He hugged me back.

"Hey!" Roddy said. He was scowling.

"Better get used to it," Ted commented.

"Roddy," Ellen spoke gently.

He turned.

"When you go home, I want you to arrange to see a doctor immediately. I'm sure your Aunt Marian will know a good one."

A stubborn, angry look came over his square face.

"I know how you feel," Ellen said. "Unique, in some horrible way. But you're not. And you're not alone. Some pretty distinguished people have had your problem."

"That's right," Ted said. "Caesar had epilepsy. So did Alexander the Great. And Napoleon. We had it in history."

"And St. Paul and Socrates, and the great composers Handel and Tchaikovsky."

"For real?" Roddy said.

Ted smiled. "For real."

Ellen said wonderingly, "Now that I know whose son you are, I wonder why on earth I didn't see it before—except that my eyes are not as good as they should be. You're exactly like your father."

Roddy's scowl cleared a little. "Thanks."

"It *is* a compliment. He's a wonderful man. I hope you value him."

"We do," I said.

"Miranda," Roddy said, as she wheeled her chair in, "our father's the red knight."

At that point she stunned us. "I know. Why do you think I let you in the first time?"

"Well, why didn't you say something?" I asked.

"Because I wasn't ready to. If you had understood

about the paintings . . . but you didn't. Your vibrations weren't right."

Ted put his arm around me. "Her vibrations are just fine, Miranda."

Ellen looked at her daughter. "Do you mean to say that you knew—or guessed—that these were Geoffrey Smith's children, and you didn't tell me?"

"I don't have to tell you everything. You don't tell me everything." She looked at me. "Your vibrations are improving," she said. "I was going to tell you."

"Roddy—" Ellen said.

"It's okay," he said. "I'll go to the old doctor."

"You can't hide, truly."

"Come on, Roddy," I said. "Let's go home. Let's walk with Ted back to the beach."

"Okay." I saw his square shoulders stiffen. "Let's go."

We walked back, one of my hand's in Ted's, the other in Roddy's.

"I'm sorry about your being fired," I said to Ted.

"It's all right. He'll probably have learned the truth by tomorrow and will hire me back. He's done that before. He's very excitable, but he's basically a good guy."

"Who do you think put in the item?"

"I'd like to think it was Larry, but I'm prejudiced."

I giggled a little. "Why would he do it? I mean, how would he know? Nobody else on the beach seemed to know who we were."

"He's big friends with your cousin Robert, isn't he? He probably put two and two together. And rumor has it you gave him the frozen mitt—you rejected him."

"He's a creep," I said.

"I think he was as appalled as anybody at what happened when the TV people appeared, particularly when Roddy—" Ted glanced at Roddy. "Sorry. That was stupid, I didn't mean to mention it."

"Well, it's there," Roddy said defiantly. "I have seizures. Ellen says I can't hide. I guess she's right."

I squeezed his hand. After a minute he squeezed mine back.

"Are you going to go in for this love stuff?" he asked.

Ted answered before I could. "I'm afraid so, Roddy. That's the way life and the rites of passage are. You'll get there, too, you know."

"I guess so."

It was as we were getting near the house that I saw the three kids who had been on the beach when Roddy had his seizure. This time, instead of bathing suits, they had on shorts and shirts and were playing with a Frisbee.

"Hi," one of them, the boy, said.

Roddy looked at them. "Hi," he said in a voice I knew well. I could almost see his defenses going up.

"Catch!" the boy cried.

For a second, as the Frisbee sailed towards us, Roddy froze. Then he put up a hand and caught it.

"Come on," the kid said. "Let's play."

For one more minute Roddy hesitated. Then he said, "Okay," and ran towards them.

"He'll be all right," Ted said. "He's got plenty of guts."

"Yes. He will."

I was very happy about it. But the happiness contained a little pain. There would always be something special between Roddy and me. But because of Ted, and because of some decision about himself that I knew Roddy had made, I realized that the kind of closeness we'd always had would never again be quite the same.